THE UNFAMOUS FIVE

THE UNFAMOUS FIVE

NEDINE MOONSAMY

© Nedine Moonsamy
First published in 2019 by Modjaji Books Pty Ltd
www.modjajibooks.co.za

ISBN 978-1-928215-80-6 (Print)
ISBN 978-1-928215-81-3 (ePub)

Edited by Karen Jennings
Cover artwork and lettering by Rudi de Wet
Book and cover design by Monique Cleghorn

Printed and bound by XMegadigital
Set in Minion

For Ma
For Kama

The children would see about the debt.
But the debt remained.

– V.S. Naipaul, *A House for Mr. Biswas.*

History of Lenasia

Lenasia is a large Indian township south of Soweto in Gauteng Province, South Africa. It has now become part of the City of Johannesburg. Lenasia is located approximately 35 kilometres south of the Johannesburg central business district and 45 kilometres South of the Sandton central business district.

Apartheid-era planners situated the group area for Johannesburg's Indians near the Lenz military base. The name "Lenasia" is thought to be a combination of the words "Lenz" and "Asia". The Lenz in question was one Captain Lenz who owned the original plot on which Lenasia is situated. Many of its early residents were forcibly removed under the Group Areas Act from Fietas, a vibrant non-racial area close to the Johannesburg city centre, to Lenasia. As segregation grew, it became the largest place where people of Indian extraction could legally live in the then old Transvaal province.

It is a testament to the people who were abandoned here by the apartheid government, that Lenasia is now a vibrant and thriving community.

✳ http://www.lenzinfo.org.za/old_lenzinfo/ourcity/historyoflenasia/

EARTH

June 1993

The front gates of Kumari's home are like metallic jaws that swallow each of her friends upon arrival. It is a house of metal and steel, with locks on the front gate, back gate, front door, side door, back door, and the pen that holds the dog when visitors come. The state-of-the-art alarm system has recently been complemented with a ream of barbed wire that now trims the top of the fortress like piped icing around the edges of a square cake.

"Come in! Come in," she squeals.

She can barely contain her excitement. Her efforts to make new friends at school have finally paid off. She has invited them to have a picnic in her garden and, by some miracle, they have all accepted. While most teenagers prefer to sleep in during the holidays, this is not the case for the Five who have already decided to keep regular school hours. It was agreed upon after Janine confessed that she will be pretending to go to school all the same.

"Hey Janine, nice uniform," laughs Neha. "I would have thought Devon would be the one to wear his school uniform during the holidays since he likes that bleddy blazer of his so much."

"Oh, fuck off," says Janine. She tries for her most playful tone but, as always, her words come out more aggressive than she expects and put a quick end to Neha's retorts.

"Ja, fuck off, Neha," Devon choruses, far less convincingly.

He has recently transferred from a private school located in the plusher and whiter suburbs and, although learning that blazers are no longer required uniform, persists in wearing his, much to the amusement of his friends.

"You know, I've been thinking," says Shejal just as Kumari gestures towards her garden, "can't we go out instead?"

"And do what?" Neha snorts. "Dude, we live in Lenz. Hardly the place for adventures."

"Ja, sure, we not going to discover anything great in the streets, but at least we can take a walk or something – just get outside!"

They eye each other hesitantly, replaying their parental advisories in their minds: none of them are allowed to go out on the streets.

"I think that would be cool," says Janine, already in gross violation of her parental constraints. "But where?"

"What about Top Shops, and then Suicide Valley?" says Devon.

"Suicide Valley?" says Kumari. "You can't be serious. That place is supposed to be dangerous."

"Let's put it to a vote, okay?" says Devon. "Everyone who wants to take this picnic to Suicide Valley, raise your hand."

Only Kumari keeps both hands at her sides, aware that Elina, her family's domestic worker, might fret and tell on her. But she quickly reconsiders; Elina is good at keeping her secrets.

"So, that's it! Let's waai," says Devon, who has been trying to pick up local slang from the rest of the Five. But it is still uncomfortable on his tongue and makes everyone smile at his effort.

"The Five go to Suicide Valley," announces Neha.

Janine scoffs. Even though Neha has explained the story many times, she is still clueless as to what those five simple characters – no doubt she is the dog – that Enid Blyton wrote about have to do with their lives. *This is the problem with books,* she thinks. Reality suffers under the gaze of people who read too much and then read too much into life.

There is no book that will make her life better, no book that will change her father, her mother, the way her food tastes and the manner in which a dog barks. She pities Neha, whose literary capacities are overdeveloped to the point of delusion. For the rest of them *Romeo and Juliet* is merely a school setwork to endure, but for Neha it has come to reflect the inner workings of her latest crush. She has walked them through it point by point: yes, they can all see the feuding families, the Hindu girl and her Muslim love interest. But if these star-crossed lovers were ever found dead, they imagine that there would only be gossip about drugs or brain-washing. Unlike Neha, they remain doubtful about whether a love of this kind can heal the unspoken animosities or the polite non-mixing of these very different religions.

When they set out from the house, they walk all along Rose Avenue, a peculiar rose with its long and straight arrangement of petals. Shejal clutches Kumari's wicker picnic basket awkwardly as they move quickly on this street; a main vein that connects the residential areas to Top Shops, mothers to groceries, young people to fast food and domestic workers to taxis. A relative, a family friend, might see them and pull them back into captivity. Janine feels the most vulnerable in her uniform; a readymade invitation for a bored patrolling policeman. Who would believe her innocence? Who would believe that she has very little that resembles a casual wardrobe, that her parents don't even know when her school holidays are and that they have never asked?

A dishevelled man walks in dizzy loops. He crosses their path and the sour stench of stale beer lingers in the air in front of them.

"Ah, hallo, Jocelene. Jocelene, hallo," he slurs.

"Uh, hello, Uncle," says Janine, mortified as her friends' surprise settles on her.

"Joh, who the fuck was that?" says Shejal when the man staggers away. "Eish, you know some hardcore characters, Janine."

"Jocelene," laughs Neha.

"No seriously, *who* was that?" asks Shejal. He has never come that close to a homeless person before.

She looks up at each of them, their polite faces turned away. She knows they are all equally hungry for a dirty tale; a glimpse at a world that their parents have probably warned them about.

"He's Alkee Uncle. He stays in the same road as me, or used to stay in the same road. But then his wife threw him out and now he has taken a vow to drink himself to death until she takes him back. He doesn't eat, just drinks, for breakfast, lunch and supper."

"Why did she throw him out?" asks Neha.

"Cos he was drinking," says Janine, "but maybe it's cos she wanted to be with that coloured man who now stays there with her. Who knows."

The Five finally reach the very end of Rose Avenue and pass through the station market of vendors, taxi drivers and travellers. They weave through the street-side fruit and vegetables; the bananas, oranges, to-matoes, cabbages, smelling both rancid and ripe. They are laid out on colourful plastic plates, measured into fixed prices of five rands. There are chicken feet and mielies roasting on fires made inside old oil drums. Large women covered in printed blankets nurse their flames. Ripples of heat float through the air and turn the world into wavy sheets of plastic. They try hard not to lose each other as their eyes feed on the spectacle of chaos, dirt, life and poverty. They cruise amongst the stalls; cheap plastic combs, aprons for domestic workers and frilly dresses for little girls in small, medium and large. They pass a makeshift tent with a hairdresser inside. The buzz of the electric razor never pauses. A board full of painted illustrations of the kind of haircuts one can receive inside stands at the front. The Five stop to look at the beheaded portraits of black men with their neat, cropped sponge-tops.

"All of those haircuts look the same," Shejal laughs.

"Well, there isn't much they can do with *their* kind of hair," says Kumari, who secretly sympathises with the stubborn curl that sprouts on African heads. Her curly, dry bush of hair is nothing like the graceful, whip-in-the-wind manes of Janine and Neha. She is the unfortunate kroeshaar of the family, as her grandmother is so fond of pointing out. Kumari constantly wears her hair in a tight bun of necessity and shame. It is to train her hair into new thinking and to hide its wicked rebelliousness, just like those men who shear their hair into nullities, never letting the sponge spew out into fully-fledged Afros.

They continue walking until they reach "the toppest of Top Shops!" Neha announces it theatrically, in contrast to the lacklustre scene. A mangy dog pees on a single, drying rose bush in front of the local post office whose red and blue façade is as cracked and faded as the face of a cheap clown.

"Joh, this is so swak," Kumari pouts.

"Argh, never mind … there's still Suicide Valley to see," says Devon.

"Ja, come," barks Shejal as he starts marching ahead down Lenasia Drive. "Let's go gang! Let's go." He claps his hands to get them to pick up the pace.

Once the houses have all but disappeared from view, the stretch of dry veld opens up in front of them. Kumari begins to shiver as the winds lick the fresh sweat from the back of her neck. "Shej, didn't your mother warn about Suicide Valley?" she asks him in a whisper directed straight into his ear.

"Of course she did, but you should know better than to heed my mother's warnings by now," he says as he drags her by the arm. "You'll never go anywhere."

"Who died here anyways? Did anyone *really* kill themselves here?" asks Neha. "It's probably all bull."

"Are you kidding me?" says Janine. "Come, I'll show you where it was done."

She trots ahead of the group as if smelling a trail. She brings them all to a high chain-link fence that circles the quarry. Their fingers spill through the holes as they fasten themselves to it, staring down into the muddy water. The fence creaks and bends under their weight; they sway along the border of life and death.

"But what could possibly make you drown yourself?" asks Kumari.

"Ja, well, people were poor in those days," says Neha. "I mean, if you poor, how else would you commit suicide? No pills, no gun, just good old-fashioned drowning."

"Oh ja, and Indian people were dirt poor in those days, neh?" says Kumari, the history of a struggle just dawning on her.

"Ja, so poor and they would still have twenty thousand children," says Devon with a laugh.

"Oh God, you should hear my father's stories about how he had to walk two kilometres with no shoes just to get to school because they were so poor and he had so many brothers and blah, blah, blah…" says Neha.

"Eish you should hear my granny's stories! She's even worse. She's got some about how she had to collect cow dung just so that they could use it to cook," laughs Shejal.

Janine watches the rest of them giggle at these anecdotes, but like Neha's father, like Shejal's grandmother, she knows there is nothing funny about being poor. "I wonder how many people died in here," she says, still stuck to the fence like a fly in a web. "And why."

A wretched wind begins to blow. In the open field they are left exposed to the blasts that howl around them. The reeds in the swamp begin to whip wildly against each other. The birds scatter in disarray and dart above the Five in a panic of having been evacuated without notice.

"Have you guys heard any actual stories about people who died here?" asks Kumari as she tries to forget the little swallows that swoop around her head.

"*I* heard a story," says Shejal.

"Cool, tell us!' beams Neha, already digging into Kumari's picnic basket for a snack.

"I heard that there were these two lovers who weren't allowed to be together so they came here to kill themselves so that they could spend eternity together. That's why they say you should never come here with someone you love or else your love will be cursed for the rest of your life."

At this Janine places her hands on her chest, just over her heart. Neha gives her an odd look, thinking it is only Kumari – or Devon – who could be touched by such a sentimental story.

Kumari fusses with the wicker basket, daintily pulling out a blanket to cover the tough burnt grass patch. Making a demonstration of her impeccable planning, she arranges disposable plates and cups with a flourish. Her mother's biryani is still warm in the small stainless-steel pot. She unties the dish cloth that keeps the lid in place. Janine hands out neatly-wrapped foil parcels to each of them as if they are Christmas presents. For the first time, she is allowed to give as everyone else gives. Now she is a part of an exchange – a friendship – and less of the stray dog in need of charity. She tries to savour the moment; the puzzled looks on her friends' faces, the thank yous on their lips.

Neha digs in her bag, not willing to let her contributions get lost in the flood. "Ta-daa! a bag of marshmallows," she announces for attention. "Ta-daa! A two-litre bottle of Coke … Ta-daa! A whole packet of black balls *and*," she holds them in suspense, "a soccer ball, stolen from my brother! Oh, bugger you all, I thought the soccer ball was a cool finale," she says, seeing their expressions fall.

"Joh, larney food," says Shejal as Devon pops the lid of his Tupperware with pride. He scans the array of crackers, cheeses, cold meats, sliced baby gherkins, bright red baby tomatoes and pitted black olives.

"And don't forget, there is Grapetiser to wash it down," Devon adds, thoroughly pleased with his work.

"Oh, and don't worry about my biryani, it's veg, Shej," says Kumari. She giggles at the rhyme and earns herself a high five from Neha.

"Ja, mine is veg as well," says Janine. "I thought it best for us all to eat the same food instead of making something separate for you … Not that it's a *big* deal or anything."

"Thanks, guys. Shej the Veg thanks you all for letting the animals live a day longer by *not* devouring them." Then taking a bite, he asks Janine, "What is this?"

"It's a creamed corn and cheese tart," she says shyly.

"Aaah man," says Shejal, "my favourite, how did you know I smaak corn?"

"And the lunch tin?" asks Kumari as she knocks on its lid.

"Well, that's for dessert. I made it myself too. It's chocolate cake."

"There is *no* way, no way you made *this*," says Neha, urgently opening the tin. "Huh-uh, no. Voetsek!"

"I told you all that I can cook. I've been cooking since I was 10. I told you guys, but you didn't believe me," says Janine with a song in her voice, shrugging off the attention.

"Oh, come on, woman. Who the hell cooks when they 10 years old?" asks Kumari.

"Ja, my sister is 10 and she is useless except for watching cartoons," says Shejal.

"Well, I didn't have K-TV," says Janine, "so I had time to learn how to cook."

Shejal is already digging in to the chocolate cake. Janine can hear a faint sigh escape from his throat. The chocolate on his chin she finds beautiful. She adds the image to her collection, wrapped in the delicate, red tissue paper pockets of her heart. *How long*, she wonders, *until it all pops out like a messy, overstuffed sock drawer.*

"You know, I have a story too," says Devon. "But I heard it from this crazy aunty who stays across from us, so don't ask me whether it's true or not. When I was small, she told me a story about this mother and her children. The story was that there was this mother in the ol' days who couldn't feed her children. So she brought them here and they all innocently dived in because she said she would send the rope ladder down after they finished swimming. But it turns out that she left them there to drown because she couldn't face having them starve to death."

Everyone remains silent as they imagine those children trying to claw their way up the muddy walls.

"Ja," Devon continues, "and I've heard from lots of *other* people who came around here that they got stomach cramps or started feeling a little sick cos those hungry children were trying to remind them of their suffering."

"I'm full," says Shejal as he throws down half a slice of Janine's chocolate cake. Soon everyone follows suit, dropping the last bits of their picnic on their plates.

"We can leave the leftovers," says Kumari. "My granny always says that it's good to feed the dead." She scoops up all the leftovers into a huge pile on a single paper plate, walks toward the quarry and leaves it just beside the fence for the ghost children.

"Oh, haha," she says as she walks back and her friends all stare past her shoulder with looks of utter surprise. "I know there's nothing behind me."

But they do not relent and she is forced to turn around just as the reeds start to quiver. The Five watch with bewilderment as an old black man strolls out from one of the dirt paths that have been tramped through the bushes by people taking shortcuts from Soweto. He spots the plate of food beside the fence and goes to pick it up. After he smells it and deems it satisfactory, he begins to eat, continuing to walk ahead. He goes straight past them without a word or glance.

"Well, Kumari, you didn't get to feed the dead, but at least you got to feed an old, hungry man," says Devon.

They begin to leave, but further up the path they retreat behind a thicket of reeds.

Three Indian boys dressed in African-American-inspired clothes – baggy jeans, over-sized football shirts and baseball caps – square off against the man in his torn T-shirt and faded brown pants. He stands in the centre of the circle. Bits of chocolate cake, cream crackers and the single paper plate fly about as they shove him from one to another. The pace is increased and the man grows stiff like a pole. It begins to look like that game where young boys toss around an old fluorescent tube light until someone drops it, releasing its gas to the heavens. Soon the boys break into a chorus of jeers.

1: "Hey old man, old baas. Stay in your homeland."
2: "Ja, old baas, don't come shit on our land."
3: "Voetsek, voetsek! Don't come shit on our land!"

1: "You still a black man, a dirty kaffir!"
2: "Ja, still the same. You think you different now?"
3: "Voetsek, voetsek! You think you different now?"

1: "Tell your kaffir friends. Tell your kaffir friends."
2: "Ja! Go home. Go home, tell your kaffir friends."
3: "Voetsek, voetsek! Go tell your kaffir friends!"

What has been a game all at once becomes something much more sinister. Two of them pin the old man's arms back and the third one takes out a switchblade, burying it deep inside his belly.

"Oh my God, we have to get out of here," Devon whispers.

The Five grab hold of each other and try to turn away, but the old man makes no sound and it is impossible to ignore the aggressive motion of the knife entering him again and again.

"Quick, this way," says Shejal.

They go right on Nirvana Drive West and run along its hideous hair-pin bend. They hear the stomping of a heavy train moving towards them and the electricity clicks madly in the overhead lines like an angry black woman moaning about the weight of her work. The train approaches alongside them and they are caught up in a net of dust. A sequence of open carriages runs past them like shutters, each carriage holding a generous load of black men who peer out at the world as it slips by; leaving Lenasia – moving out, running away, escaping – perhaps to tell, to tell their friends! When the train passes, a vacuum presents itself and the banal sounds of residential life creep back in – hooters, dogs, TVs and radios. They cover the hole, but do not fill it.

Shejal leads the way, taking the first inroad that he finds. They slip into narrow Cuckoo, left into Swallow, right into Duck, down Canary, left into Link Road. He wonders when he began to master these streets. Now in a flurry, they walk all around the Lenasia Stadium and it is only at Hummingbird Avenue that the streets begin to look familiar again. They cross over into Protea Avenue and run down this stretch before they disperse like shrapnel in their different directions.

Kumari stands outside the front gate, her fingers fumbling with the keys as with a Rubik's cube.

"Shit," she mutters, struggling to grab hold of any of them. "Shit." They all look the same. "Shit!" she screams, trying the lock. It's the wrong key!

She's only recently been given the keys, now that her parents find that she is old enough not to lose them. That was the sign to both her and Elina that Kumari can take care of herself. Elina is no longer obligated to be around after school to let her in, to make sure that she has her lunch and to check that she does her homework. A striking moment of independence that has turned the house into a cold shell.

"Elina! Please open the gate for me," Kumari pleads, banging loudly, wanting more than anything to be received by her.

But Elina does not come.

Feeling her jelly legs and quivering fingers, feeling her eyes swelling with pain as they hold back tears, Kumari remembers the numbers – the nail polish numbers! When she was given the keys, her mother dexterously painted them on the panel of each key with bright red nail polish so that she could learn the sequence. Most of them have already chipped like dried blood, but faint outlines remain on a few. The first click reassures her as she makes her way inside through all the other doors and locks.

She rushes. It is five minutes before her aunt will arrive to drive her to dance class. Ever since she was 4, Kumari has diligently attended Bharatanatyam classes. Stifling her tears, she pulls her white salwaar kameez from the cupboard. It doesn't feel right to go to her dance class today. But once she is dressed, the costume becomes something to hide behind, a wall to cement her jelly legs in. If she can dance through a story of antiquity, she thinks, the story of today will turn into a fragment so small that it will soon become completely invisible.

There's faint scratching at the kitchen door. She opens it for her little black Maltese poodle.

"Raja," she whispers, combing the wads of silky fur with her fingers.

She can hear the TV blaring from inside the Wendy house. The door is open and she walks over, but Elina is fast asleep. The sight of her body splayed out across the bed, her torso fully exposed to an intrusive beam of sunlight, sends shivers through Kumari's body. *What audacity to feel so safe on a day like this!* She goes to shake her out of oblivion, but a car hoots in the driveway and she leaves with a start.

She slaps a congenial smile on her face as she gets into her auntie's powder-blue Datsun. Her twin cousins, Prabashnee and Subashnee, are in the car. Kumari joins Subashnee, the youngest by four minutes, on the back seat. She can feel half-moons forming under her arms. She looks at the house where she has left Elina in dreamland as her aunt reverses. *There is so much to protect*, she thinks, *no wonder we have all these gates between us and the world.*

Neha and Devon walk the last blocks together and part in a silence they have never known before. Neha's eyes pierce out at the world like a stunned insect. She does not trust the dark spaces behind them anymore. Everyone has a better-than-average house on this side of Lenasia, but the gaudiness all along Seal Crescent cannot mask what she has seen today. By the time she makes it to her own home, her big eyes have become expansive dams. She rings the doorbell that plays "Nkosi Sikelel' iAfrika", and Deepak opens the door with an enthusiastic swing.

"Aaaw, Stringbean," he teases, seeing her tears. "Did Georgie Porgie make you cry?" But he quickly realises that this is about much more than pudding and pie. He folds her in his big arms. Soon Jayesh joins them, and both brothers wrap around her like the two sides of a wrench, holding tight onto the tiny bolt of her body. They accommodate every rock and sway of her frame, never letting any of its edges fall out of their firm grip. When she started high school, her father was adamant that she should join a private school outside of Lenz, but she would have had to travel with him to Parktown every day at the crack of dawn and only return well past sunset. That would have meant never getting to spend time with her brothers … and now with her two giant helpers cementing her to the ground while they wait for their parents to rush home, Neha feels grateful that she has kept this afternoon nest intact.

They are still standing in the passage, like new-born chicks saving and sharing heat, when their parents arrive. After calling the police, her father pulls a chair from the dining room and plonks Neha on it like a puppet. He holds her shoulders back so that she will not crumble forward. She looks at the family of faces as they all crouch at her feet.

Everyone has always said that Neha should have been a boy. Her tiny face is a negligible spot dropped amongst the folds of her always baggy attire. Her unruly hair is like a small frightened animal. As of late, just like her brothers, she has taken to wearing black clothing and playing the drums, listening to hard rock and heavy metal. What her parents hoped was no more than a phase continues without any signs of decline. She is steadily turning into their third son.

But Neha will remember this picture, these four faces staring at her with pity, as the moment when everything changed and she became a girl – in need of protection.

✳

When Devon parts from Neha, he walks on, uttering the only word that comes to him: "Mummy… Mummy …" He chants it like a mantra, and when he gets home, it is there – fulfilled.

His mother sits in the lounge. Her outline made luminescent by the sun that blesses her with a premature halo. She sits in the La-Z-Boy with a blanket over her legs, staring into space. Months ago, when the first tumorous pebbles appeared, she tried to attack them by prying them out of all their hiding places. She consulted with doctors, priests and lawyers to gain full comprehension and consolidation about her rights and her reality. She came back with sheets of paper copied from heavy textbooks in the library. The words of death highlighted on every page. But after a while, she put aside the papers, and began to spend her time seated like this, waiting to die.

Now she looks at him and sees her only son eclipsed by a cloud. He falls at her knees, "Mummy ..."

She closes her eyes and puts a hand on his head in an act of prayer.

"I saw a man die ... a black man, an old man. Some boys, they stabbed him over and over again. Mummy. He is dead in the field, in the field, he is dead!"

For the first time, he feels relief. This house that is so full of death gives him the voice to scream out at it, a legitimacy to speak its name. For it is there, everywhere, inscribed in the furniture, the bricks, weaved into the blanket on his mother's knees and mostly in her distant eyes. It is an easy word, a noun made common through its frequent use, and he finds liberation in spitting it out like vomit.

When she had the strength, his mother used to drive herself to church. But, defeated by the incessant weakness and gnawing pain, the weekly dose of the communion is now brought to her instead and Father Kader has become a regular in their home. Tonight, though, her insistence is high, and when Devon's father says, "I really don't think it's a good idea to take him to church, we should go to the police first," she replies, "Church is the *only* place for him now. How else will he let go of what happened? This kind of cruelty is the work of the devil! The church first, and if the spirit moves him to go the police, then we will take him."

He sits among the paltry congregation of coughing old ladies who smell like Vicks, and who all give him lips like walnuts to kiss during the Peace. The Wednesday night services seem to be the test of faith in which very few succeed at the Anglican Church. Through the hymns and prayers, the kneeling, sitting and standing, Devon cannot remove his eyes from the man at centre stage: pinned to his crucifix, his head and hair is that of the defeated. Yet Devon sees something heroic in the tensely strung ribs that stick out like armour. And those arms, spreading up and out, spelling 'V' for 'Viva!', 'V' for 'Victory!' The silent shouts from the grave of an old black man who died like a collapsing bird. Maybe Jesus, who knows this experience of humiliation and death, can see the old man, still stitched inside Devon's closed eyes. But what about the alchemy that makes him rise like a God? Is that actually something he can learn in here? And if so, what will that take?

✳

Shejal reaches home and forgets to remove his takkies before entering. There are no shoes allowed inside this double-storey house where there are carpets everywhere, save for the kitchen, bathroom and the maid's quarters in which their inclusion would be nothing short of ludicrous. They are part of the legacy of the carpet shop the family owns in the Oriental Plaza, the House of Carpets, first run by Shejal's grandfather, now by his father … and so it is expected to continue. With time their home has become an unwitting museum for defective off-cuts and pieces that just didn't sell. Each room is an idiosyncratic carpet collage; tiger prints mixing with zebra stripes in the dining room, cherry blossoms with polka dots in the lounge, and bright mustard with soft peach in the TV room. It is a house of exaggerated opulence – a kind of softness that is much too loud and that threatens to trip him up as he runs to the bathroom.

He shuts the door, pulls off his pants and sits on the toilet. Out there, outside, those streets are as terrifying and twisted as his intestines. His bowels exhale with a scream. Sweat trickles down his face. He hangs his head and stares at the rug beneath his feet, his toes digging into its blood-red fibres. He wipes himself with the commitment of a drunk, then sprawls out on the cold tiles. His wet skin touches the floor with a distinct slap, a seal arriving out of its pool. He lies with his pants around his ankles, his underpants around his knees. He tries to pull his shirt away to expose more of himself to the floor. His hot breath condenses on the tiles in front of him.

A hammering at the door brings him to his senses. His mother calls, "Shej? What is happening? Open the door!" He can already hear the anxiety in her voice.

He staggers up and off the floor and dresses himself as best he can. He calmly opens the door and steps out. He will not feed her hysteria.

"Shej!" She looks down at his feet. "What is happening to you? Why are you wearing your shoes in the house?"

Shejal turns on his heels and heads to the kitchen. He sits down at the table and waits for her to do the same.

"As I was walking home today, I saw a black man being murdered." He shoots these words out like darts – sharp and direct.

"Oh God, are you on drugs? I knew I shouldn't let you do what you want during the holidays, I *knew*. From now on you must just stay inside, stay here with me and be safe."

"God. Are you listening? A *man*! I saw a *man* die. I am not on bleddy drugs … I saw a man die, Ma."

"You serious aren't you?" She stands up from her seat to remove the divide between them, to hold her son in her arms. "Oh God, my poor child." She wraps the top half of his body with hers.

"What do I do? Go to the police?" he asks through the crook of her arm. But his mother's body has begun to shake more violently than his own and so he adds, "I guess I will wait for Daddy and then go the police …"

She suddenly retracts and stands above him, folding her arms and shaking her head over and over again. "Shej, what is that going to do? Your father works so hard and is so stressed as it is, he doesn't need to deal with these hassles. I tell you what we will do … you just forget about it and from tomorrow I will come to pick you up and drive you to wherever you need to be. I hope you learnt your lesson; you can't just be walking in the streets because you want to."

He hears a trained slamming of a door in his brain. "Ma, I swear, if you start picking me up, I *will* take drugs."

✳

Janine's body acts out a role it knows – to take her home. It is a journey that is realised through a slow change of scenery; an abundance of stray dogs, parks replaced with open patches of hard earth. The air takes on a thickness as loose grains of sand coat everything in their path; every white wall disappears behind a shroud of grey. The faces of children become darker and less well kept, and the houses becomes much, much smaller. These houses, matchboxes they're called, are an indication of the shameful municipal sham of wanting to cram as much human life as possible onto a piece of land.

She arrives at home and climbs over the short, rusted gate. This is much less cumbersome than pushing open the half-broken hinges that always threaten to fall off. The residents of Greyville fuss very little about security since they are in consensus that they have very little to protect. They have fences and gates as part of a larger aesthetic; their presence expected rather than functional.

She lets herself in and goes directly to her bedroom, draws all the curtains and stands in front of the dressing table mirror to pull off her clothes. She watches for her image in the mirror. She can see faint traces of a moving figure but nothing substantial enough to warrant the full presence of a human being. She reaches across to the dressing table and picks up a small paring knife that is otherwise hidden in a dainty pink toiletry bag with red daisies on it. On her right thigh she carves a light line with an upward stroke. Each tiny hair on her body bristles. She lies back on the bed. A warm trickle of blood rolls down her inner thigh. It is a blue of icy, unruly electricity that shoots from a stray cable and burns its unsuspecting victim into a hot, hot cinder. She shuts her eyes and lets in the blues and reds; her mind chasing the hot and the cold and making them dance in her brain. Her heart levels down and falls to a slow and steady thump.

After a while she picks herself up and pulls a tissue from the box. She collects her spillage with the care of self-preservation. The bright red devours the crisp white tissue, a liveliness that confirms the wet bloody beat of her soul. Whatever comes her way is no match for this bright-red wakefulness that throbs in her veins. Ever since she has been old enough to handle a knife, old enough to earn her keep, she has been marking these darker days. She has carefully laid the cuts out symmetrically and a veined leaf has blossomed on her right thigh. The black scar tissue rises off her skin like a drying mendhi design on the body of an Indian bride.

A heat passes under the bedroom door, a five o'clock wave with which Janine is familiar. Her eyes flick open. She hears the TV being switched on, the theme song of *Days of our Lives*. Her mother's feet rustle about on the floor – slow, then fast. She is being hunted now. With such a small surface area it is not long before her mother flings open her bedroom door. The door knocks a chair and fractures its wooden back. Backlit, her mother stands in the doorway like an omen. "So, here you are. I just hope there's food for tonight."

Janine does not move. "Ma, I saw a black man die today. I saw him bleed to death in the field."

"Oh fuck off, Janine! I'm so tired of this attention-seeking bullshit. Why can't you just carry on with life so we can carry on with ours? You saw a black man die? Guh! As if that's anything spectacular … Just get the hell out of that bed and start with supper. I'm … I'm … *tired*. I work like a fucking dog, so does your father. Just one small thing we ask of you, you ungrateful bitch."

Janine gets out of bed. She pulls on her yellow skirt and her old Mickey Mouse T-shirt and goes to the kitchen. She puts a pot on the stove and plonks in a tower of ready-made baked beans with a single thud to the back of the can. She turns the knob on the stove and melts the tower down to an even sizzle. The thick tomato gravy starts to spew up red bubbles before she turns the stove off and goes back to her room.

She counts 342 seconds before her father rips open her bedroom door. "I do not go to work, feed you, send you to fucken school and keep you in this house so you can open a can of baked beans and call it supper."

He glares at Janine who stands directly in front of him without flinching. Her face is blank except for her eyelids that beat with each passing second. He breathes in deeply, enraged by the absence of fear. He reaches for the top of his pants as if reaching for a belt, but he is caught unprepared in his elasticised blue-collar pants. He storms out and returns with the only belt he owns. She feels the lick of the leather band and hears the gold-plated tongue of the clasp sing sweetly as it rides through the air and knocks against the front of her torso. In four furious flutters of her eyelids it is done. Her father becomes exasperated by her unwillingness to collapse like a dying bird and he storms out, annoyed that he does not own a stronger, thicker and more expensive belt.

She closes the door after him and goes to her mirror. Mickey Mouse is now decorated with blood. Streaks of red soak up the lines of his smiling lips. Janine reaches under her T-shirt to touch the fresh wound, misplaced from the leaf-like calendar on her thigh. She gives a wry smile at its aptness – a day so far out of the ordinary. Her body breaks out in a fine sweat, like the ends of a camp fire being doused with water.

August 1993

Shejal has new-found autonomy at home. The autonomy of anger. His mother no longer waits for him to return from school, no longer waits for him to have lunch, nor does she try to coax him into conversation. She sees to his sister Heema's needs and then carries on with her day. In the over-productive factory of their mother's love, Heema is no longer just a silent partner.

Shejal eats his lunch in front of the TV, while Heema watches her cartoons and plays with her new puppy, Curly. Curly is Heema's recent birthday present, a perpetually happy, perpetually silly dog who will love you even when you strike him. Shejal watches his clumsy movements as he bounces around the room on his soft, unsteady legs. He has always wanted a dog. Not the Curly kind of dog, but a heroic one, the kind he has read about in books and seen on TV, nothing like this ridiculous, pink-panting pompom that flits about the room. But despite all of his pleading, Shejal never got the dog *he* wanted when he wanted it. His mother insisted that dogs and carpets could not co-exist. The initial agreement was that Curly would stay outside, but Heema has proven to be a smart negotiator. With the threat of losing the love of yet another child, his mother soon caved and granted her every request.

Shejal stares at the round flecks of hair left behind on the couches, the cushions and the carpet. They carry the subtle stink of wet fur and mud. He smirks, marvelling at the strength of his mother's wrath, that it could tolerate *this*. Curly, he can only assume, is a gift of anger and not of love, a gift for *him* and not for Heema. He smiles at the two oblivious companions; both Heema and Curly, too silly to see it, both of them happy, even when you strike them.

Out of the corner of his eye he watches his grandmother swooping past the TV room. She stops in the doorway as if she has forgotten where she is heading. He watches her snarl at the sight of the dog, and is pleased that someone else hates the thing as much as he does.

"What are you doing in here?" she shouts. "Dirtying the carpet! I just cleaned it an hour ago!"

It is a lie. They have a maid and a mother who do all the cleaning. But his grandmother yells with such fire that neither he nor his sister are willing to contest her with the truth. Heema pulls Curly against her chest.

"Calm down, Maa," says Shejal as she pulls back the pleats of her sari and falls to her hands and knees, scraping the carpet with her bare hands. But she relents when he grabs a steady hold of her and lifts her up.

"Oh Shejie, I don't understand what is happening anymore," she says suddenly.

He is startled. *She knows it too?*

"You know, there was this man, Mr Vellapan," she says in a dry voice.

Shejal sighs. He anticipates another of her stories with no more than a loose connection to reality.

"This Mr Vellapan was one of those lousy men who used to drink and talk politics the whole day. Your grandfather and all the shop owners in Kliptown, they knew how to look after their families, not running around and burning passes and getting arrested and they just left him to run out of steam."

Her eyes grow distant as she recalls the rest of it; "And to all of us, he used to say, 'You mark my words, one day, *one* day!' And now? Look at what is happening in this country… Stupid dog," she mutters as Curly cosies up to her. "Don't come shit on our carpets. Don't come shit in our house. You don't belong in here!"

Shejal breaks into a sweat, hearing echoes of the chorus of murderers in his grandmother's vehement rant. He leaves the room, terrified that she'll completely undo his attempts at drowning out the remnants of that hideous song. But even as he makes it up the flight of stairs, he can still hear her yelling and he struggles to breathe as escape eludes him.

✳

In dance class, Kumari taps out the beat with the heavy percussions of her feet. These once soft cymbals have become heavy bass drums. Over the past month her feet have begun to press these syllables into crass consonants with the weight of her uneven banging. She loses time and falls out of the rhythm set by the feet of the other dancers. Her teacher stops and looks at her quizzically. "Keep up, Kumari."

She can no longer get the moulded claps out of the arches of her feet, nor can she feign the lilting eyes of gentility.

"Dipti," says her teacher, whilst looking uncertainly at Kumari, "you try the role of Sati, and Kumari, you take the role of Shiva. Let's see how that works."

For their production of the *Thandav* it is now Kumari who gets to play Shiva; mad, angry Shiva! Her teacher makes good of her loss of lightness and she thuds about like angry thunder atop the funeral pyres in grief and silence. It is an uncharacteristic role, but if Shiva has taught her anything, it's that fiery steps are necessary too.

At home, she has taken to removing her shoes and socks to massage her puffy, raw feet whenever possible. This does not exclude the family dinner table.

Her mother admonishes her. "Dancing is supposed to be fun, Kumi.

I don't know why you push yourself so hard. Why don't you hang out with your friends anymore?"

It is only her parents, oblivious to what happened, who don't understand how radically their lives have shifted. The Five lost their taste for adventure when the streets exposed them to the fact that they were not able to be heroes when it mattered most.

"And where's Raja?" asks her father. "We don't see you playing with that dog anymore."

Kumari rolls her eyes at him. "Oh, he's just outside I guess, with Elina."

"He seems to like her more than you," he laughs.

"It's just cos she's here the *whole* day…"

She kneads her knuckles into her soles and, pressing too deeply, her blister erupts. A clear slime trickles down her foot. Her heart shivers and she breathes out heavily. Now is the time to put into action the plan she has been considering for the past two months.

"Ma," she says, exhaling again, "I didn't want to have to tell you this, but I think I have to since I saw him take it from the kitchen…"

She lets this hook dangle in the air.

Her parents rise to the occasion. "Who? What? Who took what from the kitchen?" asks her mother.

"Elina's *boyfriend.*"

"What are you talking about? She doesn't bring anyone into the house," says her mother. That is the rule.

"Oh, she *does.*"

"Kumari, just tell us what you on about," says her father.

"Elina has a boyfriend and he visits her every day and I wouldn't have said anything, but I saw him steal a knife from the kitchen today. I feel so unsafe now that I know that Elina is lying and stealing," she says quietly.

"Are you sure about this? Because I can't accuse her or ask about this if you aren't."

Kumari nods. "But don't say I told you."

"God, I can't believe we trusted her so much and she still lied to us," says her mother. "And what the hell does she want with a boyfriend? I mean, she already has *so* many children … *My God*, we just let her stay here so she can do her job, not run a whore house from our yard."

"Okay, we'll sort this out later," says her father. "Let us just eat in peace."

Her mother pushes her plate forward, too upset to eat. "I mean it's just that all her children have different fathers and now she has another boyfriend? I don't understand that nation. *Really*, I don't. If Kumari is right then we have to let her go. There is no way I'm going to let strange men roam around my yard."

Kumari bends her head at the scene she has created. *Brave things sometimes look like bad things*, she reminds herself. Elina will be sent back home. She can go and take care of her children – far away from Lenasia, where it is no longer safe for her to stay.

She strains to listen for the blare of the TV or her father's guitar. There is no sign of him. Janine hates these periods when her father, once again fired from his job, chooses to sit at home and drink instead. She eventually finds him: the top half of his body is helplessly sprawled against the toilet, with his face resting on the rim. The putrid odour is trapped in the small room, barely big enough for the both of them. She steps over his legs to flush. The stray water droplets stir him awake and he opens his eyes, but there is no indication whether he sees her or not. She bends down to stare into his face, suddenly desiring a reaction, a reaction of any kind out of him.

"Get up!!"

But he does not move or speak. Janine scoops his face into her hand. She is startled by the heaviness of it. She needs the other hand to hold it up. With this weight cradled between her palms, Janine feels a strange surge of power. There is so much she can do in this moment – she could swing it down and bring it crashing against the toilet, or the bathtub or the floor. She tries to penetrate his loose gaze, not sure what she is looking for – regret, sadness, a plea for mercy? But it is nothing, his retinas seem to have lost their shape. Janine releases his head back onto the seat and bends closer to pin his chest to hers. All her energy goes into heaving, pulling and dragging him along. She tosses his dead weight on his bed and he falls like a corpse.

✳

"Are you *girls* gonna make me play this *ninny* game forever?" Neha asks.

Since the day of the picnic, her after-school soccer sessions with her brothers have dissipated into tame ball passes on the lawn.

"Oooh, if you wanna find out who the sissy is, we can easily do that," teases Deepak.

"Yes, yes! Come on, girls, let's go," she shouts.

The brothers exchange wry smiles and begin passing the ball amongst themselves, slowly at first and then they pick up the pace. They let Neha dance around on the outskirts of the game. She re-ties her ponytail in preparation for the fight that will be demanded of her. Her eyes bulge with heavy concentration; Jayesh prepares to kick a powerful return to Deepak which she has every intention of blocking. But just as she is ready to dive and block the ball, Jayesh adjusts his step and gently passes to her. She stands there, astonished, as it slowly rolls up to her feet. She kicks in anger and it hits Jayesh in the face. His nose starts to bleed.

Deepak rushes to his aid, making him sit on the stoep with his head tilted back.

"Damn, Neha, you should really be more careful, you could have broken his nose."

"Ah, it's okay," Jayesh tries to send these words through his arched throat. "You didn't mean to hurt me. I forgive you."

"I *did* mean it, I *did* mean it!" she yells. "I *did* mean to hit you in the face."

She storms into the house, angry at having to play this delicate game. Her brothers click their tongues in pity and sigh; every action of Neha's they read, and then forgive, as a sign of her trauma.

In her bedroom, she catches sight of herself in the mirror. There is nothing heroic in her timid face, all drowned out by boy-like clothing. Would she look any better in one of those fitted school skirts like Kumari's and Janine's? She runs to her cupboard to pick out the last dress that her mother bought for her. It is a bright red dress with smocking across the top: it could fit the smallest of girls like a glove. As if being devoured by this red snake, she wriggles in head-first. She shrieks at the close contact of fabric against her skin. Instantly there is more of her to see; somehow, she seems more substantial in a dress. Neha brushes her hair back with her hands and feels her image growing almost as large as the one she has in her mind.

The August winds dip into the gaps around the wrists of Devon's white shirt. These delicate icy fingers take no heed of his navy-blue jersey and he is still cold. He walks briskly, against time, late. The bell will ring in five minutes and he has just left home. The road is quiet save for the dirty Alsatian at the end of the street. The two-toned beast barks through the red diagonal bars of the gate. Devon stops to make his ceremonial morning salutation.

"Fuck you, you piece of shit dog."

The Alsatian tilts his head accordingly and pokes his nose further out towards the road, offering a response.

"Yes, bark, you arsehole! Druk! Druk!" he says, proud of his harsh slang.

Devon chuckles to himself, wishing someone was there to witness his bravado. But he has already begun a reluctant trot, remembering the inevitability of school, and soon reaches the school fence. He pays heed to old habit, letting his fingers dip and rise in and out of the holes in the chain-link fence, and with the speed of lateness, he brings his palm to a warm flush.

The caretaker, Mr Smiley, looms, swinging the gate in a threatening fashion, exercising his authority over the influx of desperation. Devon, however, is not willing to scramble through the gate like the rest of the late-comers who are streaming in.

He is careful to nod at Mr Smiley as he enters. "Hoe gaan dit, Mr Smiley?"

Unsure of what to make of this boy who addresses him with staged formality, 'Smiley' offers him a smile.

"Mr Smiley," Devon says again under his breath and chuckles, shaking his head from side to side. He muses at his own creation, since it was *he* who christened him *Mr* Smiley. It was a toss-up between Uncle Smiley and Mr Smiley, but Devon thought that Mr Smiley had a more dignified ring to it. This, for Devon, is part of his protest against the way black men are forced to grow backwards, becoming 'boys' instead of men. In his mind, this gesture is revolutionary enough. There is no need to learn Mr Smiley's real name.

September 1993

"Well? Aren't we moving?" asks Shejal. They're supposed to be walking home together after school.

Janine stands on the spot and kicks the dry earth, watching it settle all over the tip of her shiny black shoe.

"Nah, I think I'm gonna go chill in the park for a bit. I don't wanna go home just yet, so you go ahead without me."

"The park?" He looks towards it, further down Willow Street. He has never thought of going to the park before. *Is this how she spends her time, in parks?*

Shejal draws a grading scale from sound to silence in his mind. It is a scale that begins with Neha and ends with Janine. Her silence is not the delicate shyness of Kumari that asks for approval, squeaky rather than soft. Janine's quietness leaves an impression of hardness and heat. *She is a mystery, an absolute mystery...* He wonders what it is about dark bodies that always seem to conceal themselves in veils, as if they are privy to some secret that they keep from the world. All of the dark or black people he knows are these puzzles of protest – dark and mute – the gardener, the maid, and the murdered man: he has never heard any of them speak more than five words. Dark bodies do not divulge feelings or personal information. He remembers when Francine, their previous maid, ran away, no one in the house knew enough about her to begin looking for her. It will be the same with Janine. He will never know enough to find her.

"I'll join you," he says in a panic, before a slight intimation of horror grips him as he notices her surprised smile. Janine is everything his mother is not. His mother probably became who she is as a reaction against girls like this; aggressive, poor, dark and bodied. He feels a jolt of electricity pass to him from Janine and it makes him silly with excitement. "Come," he says, pointing at the roundabout, "we can spin until we get sick!"

They jump over the painted beams that mark the boundary of the park. It is quiet and deserted and they can hear the dry grass crunch under their shoes. A flock of pigeons flies up and the rustle of wings rings in their ears.

"You go first," he offers, nudging her onto the circular base.

He grips the beam and pushes with his outstretched arms. He heaves his weight into action and sets it on a fast spin for her. The houses blend with the lawns, windows fuse into the bricks, the pigeons transform into grey smudges that dot both earth and air. The hard, inanimate steel pieces of the playground shift like fantastic animals. Sounds, too, break off from their origin and are heard out of order. Janine spins faster, the world turns before her like a pulsing vibration that pulls a long, white stroke across everything; her life inside the eye of a tornado.

Shejal folds over with exhaustion and throws himself into one of the pie-slice segments of the roundabout. He lies on his back and breathes heavily. He offers himself to the sky, his vision growing soft. Janine begins to pick off the bits of dried grass that cling to her jersey, wanting to make little of the warm breath that touches her ear.

They look away from one another. Both imagine the many eyes that must be peeping through the lace curtains of the double-storey houses that surround the park; the bored wives, the inquisitive children or the maids that draw the curtains at sunset. Overwhelmed with shyness, they pull together and trap the last sunray of the day softly between their lips.

The tips of her fingers trace the uneven bow of her mouth. She lets her fingers rest against her pout, trying to decipher the braille message that Shejal has left planted there.

Showered and changed, Devon now sits in on the visits that the priest pays to their house. Not only is he no longer cynical about his mother's religion, he is now an active participant, not missing a chance to put in an extended prayer for everything that is wrong with this world. He whispers his Our Father. He lowers his voice so that he can listen to the crisp inflections of Father Patrick's voice. Father Patrick is the new priest in charge. He studied theology while in exile in England and speaks English like no other black man that Devon knows. The Anglican Church has just recently implemented a new policy in which priests are allowed to cross the previous colour bars. It is a form of proactiveness in anticipation of a multiracial country. So, the well-beloved Father Kader has been sent off to a church in Vereeniging and the Lenasian church now has Father Patrick. But just three weeks into the job the shock is far from wearing off in the parish. Devon still giggles at the stunned old ladies who receive their communion and religious instruction from a black man. The numbers at church have fallen dramatically and it is rumoured that many of the old members now drive all the way to Vereeniging on a Sunday morning.

His mother, though, remains firm. He wonders if she would have chosen differently if she had the energy to contemplate a drive to Vereeniging. But he convinces himself that she sees it too – something special in Father Patrick – maybe he who can perform a miracle.

"I will see you on Saturday for server's practice," says Father Patrick.

He has developed a habit of ruffling Devon's hair as a parting gesture. "Ei, you Indian boys and your hair," he laughs as Devon fusses to put it back in place.

He tries his hardest to prolong these conversations with Father Patrick, but he is tongue-tied, too intimidated by this towering frame and glorious accent. He lets his hand be rocked between the giant palms as the reverend says goodnight. Devon promises himself to think of something clever to say, or ask, for next time. He cannot stand there, all teeth, forever.

"He's a nice young man, hey?" says his mother as she watches Devon bounce around the door. "I never knew I would be sent to heaven by a black man. We never understand the will of God."

※

Kumari hears Raja's nails click on the tiles. She skids down the passage to her bedroom to avoid Elina who retaliated to being fired by threatening to recite a litany of Kumari's secrets to her parents. An awareness of the breadth and scope of these misdemeanours, beginning from her childhood to the present day, compelled Kumari to come clean about lying, and Elina has kept her job. Though they have left past fights behind them, none have been as serious as this. She still doesn't know if she owes Elina a *real* apology. But she has hesitated for too long by now, wondering how one says sorry to a maid; if it is even okay to say sorry to them. She has never witnessed an apology being made to a black person before, not in life and not on TV.

"Oh God, it's just you," says Kumari shrilly when Elina enters her room, and laughs to make light of her awkwardness.

But Elina remains unresponsive while drawing the curtains.

"Oh Elina, come on man, we can't carry on like this, just talk to me!"

"You tell such big lies, Kumari," she says, her face bunched into a wounded knot.

"But you won't listen to me … I just wanted to get you home, so you can be home with your children. You don't have to stay all the way in Lenasia. I don't need you now and it is not safe for you here."

"But I work here. I make money here."

It is this reductiveness that Kumari despises the most. "Ja, but you can find work by your home. You don't have to stay here and be stuck with me when you could rather be with your children. It's your time to be free, Elina."

"But, Kumari, I work here. There is nothing at home. And home is also not safe. I must go outside for work."

"What then? Your children will come to me when they are big and say I stole their mother from them? No, I don't need you! You can go, go home to your children, what if you die tomorrow, Elina. Then what?"

Elina looks up, revealing a face pressed into a hard rock. She crosses her arms and leaves without a response.

Neha sighs indulgently as "Nkosi Sikelel' iAfrika" rings throughout the entire house. Her father has a set of keys, but gets a kick out of sharing their doorbell tune with his guests.

"Neha, my darling daughter," he announces theatrically as he leads the way to the dinner table, "meet Mr. Dlamini, Ted Dlamini," although they have met before and exchange friendly nods.

"The boys are doing well at university?" asks Ted.

"Yes, very well. It's just this little child of mine who doesn't take her education very seriously. I keep explaining to her that as an Indian woman she has to push the limits further … be brave, you know? I mean, as society would have it, all I have to do is raise her to make a decent biryani and my work is done," he sniggers.

Neha's mother walk in and slams the Pyrex dish on the table.

"Ah, Rookie! Smells good," says Mr. Dlamini. "What's for dinner?"

"Biryani!" she mutters before returning to the kitchen to fetch the rest of the meal.

"How's Aunty Thato?" Neha asks.

"Ah, she's fine, just a bit shaken up, you know. Dube is not exactly Lenz."

"Oh, Ted, come on, there is *great* unrest in Lenz. You heard at the meeting, fear is eating *everyone* alive."

"I know, but seriously, Ameet, you guys have a good deal here … Nice house, your children still attend good schools."

"Don't be so goddamn patronising, Ted," says her father, still smarting from the blow. "It's unfair to say that – we fought hard and long alongside your folk. What do you think those guys were doing? All of them, Kathrada, Dadoo, Chiba? Having a vacation in Mauritius?"

"But it's not *your* people who still have to worry about your houses being set on fire. It's not *your* mothers who still worry about food for tomorrow. A spade is a spade. Your people have always had an easier time."

"And *still* we're oppressed! It makes it even sadder, don't you think? It's all just wool over our eyes," her father replies, growing sullen. "I told you about the case we reported with Neha, hey? … I can't believe these bloody Lenz police can find a body and then shut the case because they don't have any suspects. They didn't even interview the children to ask what they saw."

The memory of that day will outlive them all. The case has been shut – but not at home.

"Neha, you promise me, if you remember *anything*, anything more that can help, you tell me. So we can get this bloody case re-opened."

Every day he asks. On some days he makes her recollect the entire incident for him, hoping to find that grain of evidence that she has so far been unable to sieve out from the sand. But unlike in books, where murders always get solved, she realises that she is a bad storyteller. The energy with which he interrogates her sucks the sap from her soul.

"At least if this case is solved," he says, "*then* we can have some resolution ... but with a police force as biased as ours – God help us!" He slams his fist against the table. "Why must we put up with this shit when we are already struggling to find our freedom? All this injustice, this *shit*, it never ends."

They are all used to the dinner-time speeches of Freedom and Change which her father delivers with the melodious optimism of a penny whistle, but the incident has dampened his tune now. The road to Freedom is no longer painted in the victorious lacquer of green, black and gold. Instead it is tainted with anonymous dead bodies that must be cleared out of the way before they can even think of proceeding forward.

November 1993

Her funeral was already planned. She personally chose the pallbearers, hymns, undertakers and caterers. There is very little left for Devon and his father to do that can count as distraction. They sit in their suits next to the coffin that his mother chose for herself. The air is thick with incense and Devon's father winces as he hears the heavy coughs that come from people's clogged chests. There are no hideous signs of grief: no howling, wailing or fainting; no unreasonable demands being made of the corpse. There are just the subtle sounds of awkwardness; mothers shushing their children, sweet wrappers crinkling in discreet palms and the whispering from one ear to another about other people's misfortunes.

Shejal, Janine, Kumari and Neha shuffle about; none of them have ever been to a Christian funeral before. Janine has never been to any funeral and imagined it to be like something in *The Bold and Beautiful*. As she looks at the ladies in their formal dresses and the men in their dark suits and silky ties, she sees that she is not completely wrong. They edge forward, in a bunch, towards Devon. None of them will look into the open coffin. Only Janine, full of curiosity, peers into the frigid face of death. This, her first funeral, fills her with a strange sensation of floating. Is this not what they are all doing, floating through the world? How real, how inevitable; nothing, no one, is immortal – everything dies. The thought alone makes her giddy.

"Daddy?" asks Shejal tentatively as he spots his father outside the church.

"Shejie," his father says, "I left work early to get here."

"Oh, of course, you know Devon's father from the Plaza."

"Yes, he has had his shop in the Plaza for a long time now."

Shejal remembers how he used to spend his school holidays in his father's shop, sitting on the carpets all day, imagining that they would grow wings and he would fly away to some great destination. "Funny how I never bumped into Devon at the Plaza, hey," he says.

"It's okay. You will meet there when you take over from us." He laughs at his little quip, but a bitter taste fills Shejal's mouth as he thinks of those stupid carpets under which his father wants to bury him.

Janine loiters behind him; too scared to go forward and introduce herself. Ever since their first kiss, he has coolly ignored her in front of their friends, as if it never happened. She imagined that some declaration of love was bound to follow, but she is slowly being trained out of that idea.

"Well, are you going to the cemetery? Want to come with me?" Shejal's father asks him.

"Ja, ja, I'm coming." He turns back to Janine. She was just beginning to wonder if he even noticed her standing there.

"I'll meet you at the cemetery," he says. "I'm taking a ride with my father."

He goes off and leaves her muttering, "What? Is the car full?"

She scowls as she tries to search the crowd for Neha and Kumari so that they can make their way to the cemetery together.

Neha looks out across the expanse of Avalon Cemetery. The tombstones stretch out in neat rows like a plantation. The wind whips the loose soil

49

from the graves of the recently deceased and throws it up into their faces; the delicate few hold handkerchiefs to their mouths and noses.

"Look, Kumari," says Neha.

Kumari's eyes follow her hands as she traces a huge mass of shacks that fall on the further side of the cemetery.

"Soweto," she says as she drops her hand, and waits for Kumari's reaction.

Kumari's head whips back to see how far from home they have come.

"Lenz," says Neha, to mark the space for her.

Again Kumari turns her head to the other side.

"Soweto," says Neha, reiterating how they are so literally divided by death that it is almost comical.

Kumari's head shifts back and forth, feeling vulnerable in the space. This is her first real glimpse of Soweto and she slowly falls into really observing it; the lopsided and rotting zinc roofs, the threadbare washing hanging from loose wires, the smashed together plots and the plastic packets that stick to everything. She can see it all now, from the same vantage point as the dead.

Most of the people have left by now. Devon feels relieved to take off the suit and be done with the politeness it demanded. The house feels alien with all the furniture moved about and he goes back to his room where everything still remains as it was before. There is a knock at the door.

He sighs as he braces himself. "Come in."

His mother's cousin peeps through the open crack.

"Julian, come in."

The man has not said a single word to him all day. He assumes the same "Sorry about your loss" routine is to follow. Devon tries his best to look pleasant, but is startled at Julian's appearance. The only man he thought of as eternally youthful stands haggard and aged before him. He is the only grown up that Devon has never called "Uncle". None of his cousins call him that either. He has always been a different kind of grown up in their eyes.

"Your mother asked me to talk to you," says Julian abruptly. "She called me about a month ago and said that I should speak to you, you know … after she is … gone. She wanted me to tell you," he says, hesitating with the rest of the sentence. Julian has not even sat down. He looks like a nervous actor that just wants to speak his part and leave.

"What?" Devon is starting to feel distressed.

Julian sighs and begins again. "She said that I should talk to you and tell you that … that it's okay."

"What's okay?"

"She wanted me to tell you that it's okay to be gay, and to talk to you about it."

"What! What are you talking about?" He can only laugh. He has overestimated just how old Julian has become. Here he is, playing a trick on him at his mother's funeral. "I'm not gay," he says, shaking his head.

"Just shut up and listen! Your mother asked me to do this, so I *will*. You can do what you want with it, but I'm doing this for your mother because she asked me to." The words come out in an angry burst and Devon surrenders.

"So," says Julian, "your mother wanted me to give you this whole speech about how it's okay to be gay … like I am Felicia Mabuza-Suttle or something. But you know what? I'm just gonna be honest with you. That's bullshit. Because it isn't *okay* to be gay and you just have to learn to live with that. You're not just different, you know, like a fucken black sheep or something. No, it's like being a dirty goat in the flock of black sheep that have already been cast out from the white ones. I wouldn't have got in this mess in the first place if I had people who supported me, you know … people who said 'Hey man, it's okay to be gay.' And now look, I have fucking AIDS and they still pretend like they can't see me. So all I wanna say is don't expect any support from these people, they'll just turn a blind eye when you need someone to see you." His voice drops. "I know your mother meant well, and God bless her, but what I want to say is whether you're gay or you're not gay, do it differently, not like me. I mean, I told *everyone*, like I expected some kind of party or something. God, I look back at my young days and I cringe at the person I was. I spent my whole young life laughing, pretending to laugh with them – arseholes, fuckers, middle-class hypocrites."

"I'm sorry." This is all Devon can mumble in the moment.

"Oh, don't start saying sorry… you'll end up living your whole life like an apology. Look," he says, "I know it's not what your mother wanted me to tell you. But I can't lie to you. You got a kak deal, Devon, but try your best and just carry on with your life."

He turns to the door and leaves in a hurry. Devon's eye's gloss over with astonishment. AIDS – it is one syllable too many to mention. He did not know. Why didn't anyone tell him? AIDS – a single aspirant, sharp and direct: all the violence of the world is distilled down to single syllables: AIDS – GAY – DEATH – SEX – FUCK – YES – NO – GOD. He feels each falling on him like a rock, and his body gives way to an avalanche as he collapses on the bed.

January 1994

Ever since Devon's mother's passing, the Five spend their free time at his house.

"Ja, I know, my father is becoming a bit of a slob," says Devon – their gasps are almost audible – as they enter the house. "It's so irritating. I have to do most of the cooking and cleaning up, like I'm the bleddy maid or something."

"Tell me about it, brah." Janine can only sympathise with his plight. "I'll find us some clean glasses," she volunteers, already tidying up as she heads for the kitchen. She comes back with five washed glasses, but she does not sit idle and begins to clean everything in sight.

"Maybe I should help her," says Kumari guiltily.

"Eish, she likes to play house, hey," says Neha, piqued. Is *she* now expected to help?

Yet everyone leaves Janine to her task except Kumari, who paces between the kitchen and the lounge.

"Hey… can I ask you something?" Devon asks nervously, pulling Neha into the passage.

Neha sighs as she watches the funeral gloom settle back on his face. "Of course, Devs."

"Nah, never mind. Forget it."

"Aw, Devs, you can ask me anything, we friends, come on. Come on, man ... You're the nik to my nak, the Aero to my mint, the bir to my yani, the gulab to my jamun."

"Oh shut up, now you just making me like a pop."

"At least you're smiling. So just ask me now. *Ask me*," she growls and tugs at his shirt sleeve.

"I wanted to ... no, forget it," he says, shaking his head.

"If you don't tell me, I *swear*, I will kill you."

"Shit, ja. You'll make my life hell."

Neha nods. She cannot bear not knowing a secret.

"I wanted to know if you think that I am g ... g..." he stutters.

"Grieving?"

"Huh? No, man."

"God, what then?" she asks. This is taking too long for her liking.

"Gg ... gg," he tries again for just that one word, a single syllable.

"What? Gay?" she asks, growing impatient.

The quick dart of his eyes is revelatory. "It's okay," she says, pulling him back towards her. "To be honest, it was the blazer that led me on," she laughs. "Ja, you can be just like Freddy Mercury! Cool, neh?"

Shejal pins Janine to the blue, metal framework of the swing.

"Suko lapho," says a harsh voice. They spot a black beggar, his hair matted into dreads, a dustbin bag of belongings at his feet. "Hamba," he says, clicking his tongue. He waves his arms at them for defiling his home with their lust. They stare in shame at the embarrassing places their hands have reached. As they become conscious of the warm heat between their bodies, they pull apart, moving away from the ball of friction.

"Come!" Her hand grips his wrist around his pulse point; his life is in her hands.

His heart beats fast as he witnesses the changing landscape. *She is taking me to Greyville!* Yet he follows along – the promise is much too strong. He passes it all as if falling down a shoot; the red robots turning to green, the lawns becoming sparser, the sand getting looser, the stares of curious, dirty children, the brown dog that nips at his heels, the broken gate, the faded number on the front of the house, the single bush of wildflowers that blossoms in her yard, the door that catches, and at the end of the tunnel he stumbles into the darkness of her bed.

✳

Kumari hears the sound of clanging pots and plates coming from the kitchen; the loud engine noises of her mother's uterus. Drawing closer for dinner, the smell of her mother's skin multiplies; onions and mustard seeds steeped in rich, salty butter. It drenches the room in creamy fabric.

"Oh, Raya, you've cooked my favourites!" She watches her father sneak a kiss as he takes his seat at the table.

"You say that every day. I don't even know what's your favourite anymore."

"Anything you make is my favourite," he coos and then laughs. He knows he has taken it too far.

These little exchanges usually cause Kumari to blush more than her mother. She always wondered why she didn't have a little brother or sister, but that was only until she learned about the stillborn baby that had wrecked her mother's womb, leaving Kumari as the sole benefactor of her parents' attention. Her mother rests her chin in her palms and watches her daughter scoop handfuls of rice dripping with dhal. Beyond her tired smile, Kumari notes other signs of uncomplaining sacrifice; there are chips in her fingernails and grey hairs springing out of her dyed black mane. When Kumari thinks of her family, she always pictures a bicycle. Her parents as two hard-pressed wheels and she as the seat. She understands that they grind themselves down to the ground just so that she might never need to touch it. It is her job, she knows, to keep the bicycle intact and moving forward at all costs.

✳

The sound of Father Patrick's car pulling up in the driveway makes Devon anxious although he has been waiting to be picked up by him. As his life begins to morph, as he comes closer to the inevitability of who he is, he cannot help but feel that he is betraying the close esteem of the reverend. He sighs and braces himself, having promised that today will be *the* day. Yet just the sight of Father Patrick's earnest smile is enough to unnerve him, already he can feel his resolve fading.

"What's wrong, Devon? You look rather tense."

He stops fidgeting. "Aah, had a hectic week, hey." Then admonishes himself for missing this opportunity to just come out and say it.

"Why, what happened?"

Devon shakes his head, sighs and keeps his eyes locked on his feet.

"Oh, young man, you can tell me anything. I'm sure I've heard it all before," he laughs heartily. "I sat through all kinds of confessions."

"Something is wrong with me," says Devon gravely.

"What's been happening … thinking about your mother?"

"No, *me*, something is wrong with *me*. I think I might be…" He breaks out into a cold sweat – just one more syllable and his confession will be done.

"What? You might be gay?"

Devon's eyes flare with shock.

"How did I know?" asks Father Patrick with a twinkle in his eye. "Well, before your mother died, she outed you," he chuckles.

Devon grows irritated with the genial laughter; he is confused and angered by what he is being told.

"No, no ways! I don't believe you! Why would she tell everyone else but me? I mean, she told my uncle, she told *you*, and even one of my friends said she already knew when I tried to tell her. How did everybody know before I did?"

"Maybe it's just that all of these people were ready to accept it before you were," says Father Patrick. "Your mother told me that she thought you were gay, and that I should be ready to receive you with my open arms if ever you came to speak to me about it. She was quite cheeky about the whole thing."

"So what now?" asks Devon. "Are you going to excommunicate me?"

Father Patrick looks at the stern and sombre lines on Devon's face. "The way I see it is that you need to take this with patience and prayer. I mean, just take it as it comes. If you look at the world, the definition of the outcast and the sinner is never absolute. First it was the dirty gentiles, then the Jews had a turn, and blacks and women and, well, gay people. I wouldn't make too much of it, it's just the church of God perfecting itself as it goes along." He shrugs; a disclaimer – this is his only way of explaining the tumultuous history of the church. "If being a Christian is important to you then you need not be discouraged. Don't get me wrong, you may have to fight your ground, if that is what you want. To be honest, I wouldn't be here if I didn't …"

The dinner parties at Neha's house have hit their fever pitch although the elections are still in the offing. As the day grows closer, the crowd grows larger, the drinks grow taller and the conversation louder.

Dinner has not yet been served and the men have already stopped bothering with the pretence of serious political discussion. The women listen to excerpts of out-of-tune songs from the kitchen. There is enough help for her mother today and Neha floats around the kitchen without having to get involved.

"Don't you get pissed off with all these parties?" she asks.

"Well yes, and no," says her mother. "It's a worthy cause to celebrate and I'm doing my bit."

"Your bit?"

"Yes, *my* bit. My bit for the cause. It's not the same type of jumping and skipping like the rest of the men, but ...well, it's like when a baby is born. All the men get drunk and light cigars, and the women, they just carry on breastfeeding in the nursery, all by themselves, making sure that the baby actually grows."

Neha laughs at the wry smiles of recognition on the lips of all the women. Mrs Jonson holds a piece of cheese loosely against the chopping board, too afraid to dirty her impeccably manicured hands. Neha smiles at her, out of place in a kitchen. She loves her long, liquid body, her clear and creamy complexion and her thick black curls that bounce as she sways to the music. In dumpy comparison there is Mrs Moreen Tlale. A fat black lady who hasn't even changed out of her nurse's uniform. She whips a bowl of batter, cradling the dish against her belly.

"Eish, my back is sore," she moans. "I'm on my feet all day and now I have to do this before I can enjoy the party."

"Well, we better make quickly. The party is already happening without us," sings Mrs Jonson.

"What are these men on about? They haven't even won the election yet," says Mrs Tlale peevishly.

"Ja, but it's pretty much in the bag, hey," says Mrs Jonson.

Neha looks at her mother, not bothering to join in the conversation as she flies around the kitchen, chopping, stirring, peeling, throwing and turning. She has no time for chitchat. She looks bothered and flustered and ... old. How much of her mother's life has been missed, with all of her youth wrapped up in her father's rolling speeches and her brothers' crazy antics? Nobody ever takes a moment to notice how the house manages to function on its own: that quiet miracle, she now realises, is her mother.

Her mother throws a boiling pot of rice into a strainer. The pot sizzles as its hot base touches the pool of water in the sink. Neha moves closer towards her, breathing in the smell of wet rice off her mother's clothes. She strokes her arm; the sleeve feels warm and moist as if it has just come out of a steam press.

May 1994

"Look at this mess," says Kumari as another rotting election poster comes crashing to the ground just in front of her. The Five wade through the plethora on their way to Devon's house.

"It's mad, huh," says Neha. "To think that all that hype amounts to this."

The elections passed through Lenasia like a noisy wind. The entire area was covered with posters and banners; every lamppost shedding light on a different face, a different candidate. These faces covered the fields and fences of schools and public spaces. They were on television and paraded in the streets and stadiums; people marched with mega-phones and flags, carrying badges and promises door to door. Now the deluge of democracy has simmered down to dirt as posters detach them-selves from walls and fill the gutters and clog the drains.

"So, here's to Kumari!" toasts Shejal.

They are drinking in her honour today. Not only has she graduated as a Bharatanatyam dancer, but she also performed at the presidential inauguration recently.

"Thank you all, so much," she beams.

"And *you*," Devon sings. "Wow, Kumari!"

At her graduation concert, Kumari was far from her usual plain, otherwise undistinguishable self; she became a goddess in front of their eyes.

"It was not all as smooth and slick as it seems," she says. "The chaos backstage! Joh, I had like three aunties dressing me at one time; the one sticking my hair on, the other fastening my outfit and the other putting colour on my feet. And the jewellery – it was so heavy. They had to fasten the chain to my blouse so it wouldn't slap me in the face every time I jumped," she laughs. "But it was magic," she says softly to herself as she remembers how at some point the dance started dancing itself.

"God, you waited so long for this," says Neha in awe.

"Good things are worth waiting for," says Kumari. It is what her mother always says. It is true.

"No seriously, you kicked ass," says Shejal. "You were *way* better than your cousins even though you are younger than them."

"Well, I started dancing much earlier than they did," says Kumari, to be fair, to be modest. All this praise makes her uncomfortable.

"I still don't get why they would want Bharatanatyam dancers at the inauguration ceremony," says Janine.

"Where have you been?" asks Neha. "We're the Rainbow Nation! We're celebrating our multiculturalism! It's about time everybody's contribution to the country should be seen," she continues, but quickly bites her tongue, realising just how much she sounds like her father.

"And Mandela, oh … it was amazing, just amazing," beams Kumari. "He is *so* tall, like the friendly giant, with big hands and everything – you would never notice that on TV. And, my God, he just glows. I swear, he *glows* … like you just want to melt in front of him!"

"Okay, okay, we get it," says Neha bitterly as she slurps her drink. "*You* met Mandela and we didn't. *Yay* for you!"

Kumari does not retaliate. In truth, she is scared to death of what an encounter with Neha will amount to. She *will* lose. There is too much aggression residing in that small body for Kumari to score a point of her own. She will never forget that first handshake from Neha: the strength that shot out of those frail bones shocked her like live electricity. Even her eyes are like harsh needles. They do not bend and flicker like other girls' do. They stab! Everyone feels that Janine is the dark horse of the group, but for Kumari it is Neha that they should fear the most.

"Here's to dreams finally coming true," she says as she raises her glass.

"Here, here," they chant and down their drinks.

This is the year they have all been waiting for. As matriculants they are planning the rest of their lives, dreaming about driving cars and legal drinking. The entire universe seems to take a sweet, deep breath in anticipation of their unfolding adult lives.

"You know, guys, my father said that if I pass my drivers, he will get me a car," gloats Shejal. If they have nothing to talk about, they can talk about him.

"Ah man, we can finally go out of Lenz if we have a car," says Devon.

"Finally, good grief!" chirps Neha.

"And our parents won't be on our arses anymore," says Shejal. Devon's eyes drop and Shejal feels callous for his words. Not everyone draws maps in order to get away from their parents. This is something he shares exclusively with Janine and from the corner of his eye he sees her silently toast him. "We'll get there." Shejal feels confident now that he has managed to convince his father to let him go to university, falsely promising to take over the shop once he finishes his computer science degree.

"Janine, how we wish you would come with us to Wits," says Kumari wistfully.

"Ah it's okay, brahs, money doesn't grow on trees, blah, blah blah… so I have to start making my own. And besides, I'm not like you nerds! I *hate* studying. I'm glad it's over and done with, no university for me," she laughs.

"What kind of a job will you get though?" asks Devon.

"Any kind I can find." Janine shrugs at the uncertainty.

Devon smiles, it is comforting that someone else does not have much of a plan. He is only applying for a BA degree because Neha is.

✳

"I can't believe the priest said it was okay. My father always says that organised religion is dogmatic. That's weird, isn't it?" says Neha.

"Well, ja … it is," says Devon as he runs his palm across his head. He can still make little sense of how that conversation is going to play out in his life. "But I think he meant it's okay to be gay but not *gay-gay*. You know?"

"Like what? Those ones who wear dresses and stuff?"

"Oh, I don't know. What is okay at the end of it all? I mean, the more I spend time with Father Patrick, the more I want to be like him. I don't want to be like my uncle or Freddy Mercury."

"Here," she says as she takes the broom from him, offering to help with the cleaning for the first time.

"Thanks, Neha, you're a peach. The most amazing thing that happened in my life, you know that?"

She blushes. "I'm dik excited that we going to Wits together next year."

"Ja, me too. It'll also be a good space to figure myself out, you know."

Neha walks home feeling lonelier than usual; back to the quiet house with no one to amuse her but herself. Her heart begins to swell as she thinks about Devon's life, about the lives of all the men who have surrounded her. Somehow, they all seem to have taken on a course that no longer includes her. It has happened to her father and each of her brothers in turn. Now she is losing the last man that could love her forever.

She is about to turn towards her home when she spots Shejal and Janine walking down Rose Avenue. Surely if they were heading straight home, they would have been much further along their route than this? She and Devon have noticed suspicious exchanges between them and, intent to get to the bottom of it, she hops behind pieces of sparse foliage along the street in order to keep up with them. She watches them walk past the Total garage on the left and then enter the slip road that leads into Greyville territory. *Are they going to Janine's house?* Neha looks around cautiously as she takes this bend herself. She has never been inside Greyville before. When she tries to cross the road, a black Golf with ominously tinted windows and booming speakers screeches to a halt. A string of menacing wolf whistles flies at her. She quickly jumps to the pavement, wishing she hadn't come alone now that it has brought her into such uncertain terrain.

She is shocked at the sight of the houses. She has never been to Janine's and always took it as light-hearted humour when she referred to herself as poor. The entire area looks like a big junkyard; burst tires on the pavements, fences of brittle scrap metal for chicken coops and broken plastic chairs that sit in dry, dusty yards. There are a few children around, one with mucus dribbling from his nose. She wonders what happened to the Great Indian Ingenuity that her father always talks about. What happened here?

She watches them enter a house, waits a minute, then runs across, scribbles a note, signs it and slips it under the door. She lacks the spirit to knock and scream "Ta-da!" to their shocked faces. How embarrassed they would feel, all of them.

As Neha passes Shejal's street, she stops to look at his house. She has (dare she say it?) a new-found respect for him, for being able to look past the pretentiously high arches that line the front. It's just like Romeo and Juliet. She is stung with jealousy for the simple and secretive beauty of their love. She sighs at the long, lonely walk ahead. *I am just an ant stealing little scraps from other people's picnics so that I can have a little one of my own*, she thinks. Every piece of excitement in her life is vicarious, borrowed or stolen – she has no secrets: none worth keeping, none worth sharing. *Perhaps I am just here to watch.* She can see how effortlessly, how easily, the world turns and changes without much need for her. She looks at the stream of traffic on Rose Avenue as people start to come home from work. All of these cars, full of life and stories, zip past her as she walks by, silently, on the side of the road.

✳

Janine lies on her back in disbelief as she muses at her weak resolve. She is beginning to feel diseased by Shejal, a sickness she can't shake. Maybe her mother is right – a boy can turn you into an idiot. She tilts her head onto her propped arm and peers down at him as he fights off his sleep. The soft curves of his body, his rounded back and bent legs all twist away from her. He is folded into himself. She runs her finger along the constellation of beauty spots that lie dispersed under his left ear like the trail of a comet. She makes a wish, the same wish she makes every time. She pulls her finger away from his pale flesh as her heart begins to burn. She can feel him getting restless at her touch. She lights a cigarette and blows smoke as he dresses to leave.

A few minutes later, Shejal kicks the page when he opens the front door and reads it quickly: "I know I know I know!!! I told you so that I know!!!" And below that in big letters: "NEHA."

He feels sick with shame; he knows she only pretends to like the secret for his sake.

"Neha, you shit," he mutters, thinking she is too inquisitive for her own good as he hands the note over to Janine.

✳

"Come, Kumari!" Elina is excited and Raja wags his tail as they wait for her. "You must see… it is too nice."

"Ah, Elina, can't I come later?" asks Kumari sluggishly.

But Elina pulls her by the arm and guides her out the kitchen door and into the back yard. "Come, come," she says, dragging her towards the little Wendy house.

Kumari hangs back cautiously. Now that they are barely on talking terms, this burst of old enthusiasm makes her feel sheepish.

"*Come*, Kumari," Elina moans.

She creeps in slowly. It's been so long since she has been inside. The smell of paraffin sticks to everything. She scans the contents of the room; the broken picture frame, the old vase, the discarded whiskey bottle with a fake rose in it. She has recycled all the junk of their house and spun a home out of it.

"See, see," says Elina, as she jumps on her creaky bed and points at the wall.

Kumari turns to see a photograph of her and Elina at her dance graduation.

"Big miesies gave it to me last night," says Elina.

The photo is one in a line, each showing an unfamiliar child. Kumari counts five. She looks at the photograph again and feels ashamed by the fake smile that she wears in it. She shakes her head. "You should take that down, I look stupid."

"Hayi, voetsek! Me? I'm proud," she beams, "you dance better than Brenda Fassie."

Kumari's expression leaks unworthiness. She can think of no greater compliment coming from Elina's world.

✳

Devon plonks himself in his mother's chair to make sense of the news.

"He voted in the elections," says his uncle. "If anything, that's a man signing a promise for the future."

No one thought that he was secretly dying. Neither he nor his uncle saw the signs of his father's sudden cardiac arrest. They were just as helpless as the doctors who failed to resuscitate him.

Devon floats away in his chair. His uncle's monologues grow dim. There is a white sheet of shock between him and the world. He pictures his father in the middle of all that brass and glass, sees him falling to the floor in his own store. His father's heart must have cracked like a cheap vase, shattering on the ground into a million shards that could never be glued back together.

"I just thought he was working so hard to deal with his grief…" says his uncle.

Devon feels weightless as he sees his father's face. At least his mother said goodbye, even if she spent so much of her life doing it. He thought he had mastered death, but he sees how very wrong he was. The emergency room trauma will live on forever. *What now? What now?* he wants to scream.

AIR

February 1995

"Welcome to my humble abode," says Devon.

Shejal looks past him, trying to gauge his surroundings. Ever since Devon took over his family home, the furniture moves around regularly, the curtains and pot plants shifting and changing just as often. All except his mother's La-Z-Boy that still sits in the middle of the empty lounge like a wet, black meteorite that has fallen into a dry, beige desert.

Janine runs to the door, wiping her hands on her apron and pushing back the strands of hair from her face.

"For you," says Shejal. He holds out the bunch of red carnations towards her.

"Aw, Shejie, they're beautiful," she whispers, too choked to speak.

After Neha's snooping, they have had no choice but to let go of their secret. He smiles, pleased that he can now make these public gestures that make her melt with gratitude.

"Okay, enough man," says Kumari, unable to take much of the cooing and kisses.

"Come now, you have to help me get this show on the road," says Devon, pulling Janine away from Shejal.

"Let *me* help you," says Neha.

"Uh ... just don't break anything."

"Of course I won't." She can hear Janine snort sarcastically in the kitchen.

"You have butter fingers. Just be careful," says Devon, eyeing her cautiously as she carries a stack of plates to the table. "No, no, take out the silver-trimmed ones. Can't you see it's a silver day today?" He points at the shiny overlays that he has already spread out on the table. His new love for crockery and cutlery, and every other home décor item, comes inspired by the Oriental Plaza. It is here that he discovers fine crockery and cutlery with ornate trimmings, as well as a bright modern palette of bold neon dishes cut into every imaginable pattern. He can afford this new fetish thanks to the kindness (or sympathy) of the other shop owners in the Plaza who all remember his father fondly and now let his son buy from their shops at a discounted rate.

"God, I can remember times when we used to drink out of paper cups," says Shejal.

"Sometimes out of the bottle," adds Devon, shrugging off the memory.

"Sit! Sit!" exclaims Janine as she brings in the food. "Chicken curry and roti, and brinjal curry for the vegetarian."

"Eish, wine and chicken curry," says Neha.

"Everything goes with wine," says Devon.

"No, everything goes with chicken curry," says Kumari.

"Wait!" shouts Janine. "We forgot to pray."

"You can't be serious, no man," says Shejal. This is the last thing he expects from her.

"You see what living with a priest does to you?" Kumari whispers to Shejal.

"I'm a lay minister, not a priest. It's hardly the same thing." The same mistake gets Devon flustered every time. He clicks his tongue emphatically before he rises to pray.

"Amen," sings Neha once he is done, dragging it out like the African-American gospel singers she has seen on TV.

"How's university?" Janine asks Shejal, having missed an entire week of his life. She has a lot to catch up on.

"Oh God, don't even ask," says Kumari. "The term just started and I'm so behind with work."

Shejal and Neha nod in agreement.

"Joh, I feel like a kak loser! I mean, in our maths class we have these nerds from white schools who all did extra maths tuition, so I feel like a real dof thing," says Shejal.

"It's the travelling every day that kills me the most," says Kumari. "By the time I get home, I'm so exhausted that I just fall asleep. And I'm so pissed cos my dance teacher asked me to help her teach the younger children, but I can't even make time for their classes during the week cos I just come home and I'm dog tired. Wits is taking over my life!"

"You people make me feel glad that my father stuck me in res," says Neha who now only comes home on the weekends.

"Shit," says Janine, "I thought you guys were supposed to be having the dikkest party of your life at Wits." But their three faces reprimand her for her ignorance.

"Sometimes I think I should have just taken over my father's shop," says Shejal dismally.

"No! You don't," says Devon who gave up on university to do exactly that. "No, you don't mean that, *seriously* ... I sell as much glass and brass as I can to a bunch of strangers that I can't be bothered about, and that's every single day. It never changes," he says, dragging his words to emphasise the monotony of his work.

"And *I* deal with the world's rudest people who expect you to work faster than the frikken machine can scan," says Janine who works as a cashier at Plastic Warehouse. "And you can't even swear at them, you have to smile and be polite. I could dig out their eyeballs sometimes."

Shejal pats her on the back. They all know the kind of strength it must require for her to act politely, to bite her tongue.

Devon sighs as he sips his wine. *This is the adventure of life,* he thinks, *travelling through each other's lives, each other's weeks.*

The clicks of the cutlery grow lazy and the conversation drops as everyone settles into their Sunday afternoon slump.

"Do you guys mind cleaning up?" asks Janine as she pushes back her chair. Shejal uses this as his cue to do the same.

"Go," says Devon, smiling cheekily.

"Thanks." She picks up the last of the wine. Shejal has already darted off to the bedroom.

"I still think they make an odd couple," says Kumari. "Especially because Shejal is quite the man on campus. I've made so many friends because all these girls want to know if I'm his girlfriend."

"Oh ja, I know. I got that a couple of times as well," says Neha, sticking out her tongue. "I dunno, I still think it's weird that you let them shag in your parents' bedroom."

"What?" shouts Kumari, sitting up, sober. "You mean…"

Devon and Neha widen their eyes to coax her on towards the truth.

"You mean… You mean, that they did *it*…They had sex?" she whispers, the words finally popping out of the prison of her mouth. "Have they been sleeping with each other all this time? Sex! They had *sex*? Like, *sex*-sex?"

Neha nods up and down ferociously. It is cruel but delightful to watch as Kumari's naïveté disintegrates like a crushed egg.

"Shit, why am I always the last to find out these things? God, I haven't even kissed a boy yet. And our friends are having sex together? I don't understand it. Do they even love each other? What if she falls pregnant? Oh my God…" Kumari breaks out in a hot sweat. She gets up and messily pulls the dirty dishes together to take them to the kitchen.

"We should have cushioned that a bit better for her," says Devon.

They can hear the kitchen taps roaring as she fills the sink. She stirs in the dishwashing liquid. She scrubs away the shock one dish at a time, keeping silent. They will all laugh at her, they always laugh at her. "Kumari, the old-fashioned, the aunty," they will say.

After all the dishes are done, she slumps back into the chair, feeling a little calmer.

"I'm sorry. I thought you knew," says Devon.

"Ja, me too," says Neha.

"It's fine," she mutters.

"You know, Devon and I, we also haven't had a boyfriend and haven't been kissed either," says Neha with a shrug. "So, we're like a team."

"What? You recruiting me for a team of losers?" asks Devon, and Kumari cracks a slight smile.

"Oooh," says Neha, suddenly giddy. "I met this boy in the res across from mine."

"Oh no, you leaving the team already!" says Devon.

"No man, he's a gay boy. I think you would love him. He's studying anthropology and he's so cute. He's a whitey, but we get along. He's cool."

"Oh haha, very funny, Neha," says Kumari. "As if Devon is *gay*."

Neha and Devon glance at each other.

"Oh God," says Kumari. Then, "Hey! I thought you were a priest … I mean a lay minister." She rises abruptly. "I'm going home. I should be at home, it's a family day."

"Hey, we *are* a family," says Devon, sounding a little offended. "Look, I even have a picture of us on the counter." But she is already out the door.

"I never noticed that picture," says Neha as she chuckles at their lousy matric ball outfits. "We look like dorks."

"God, Kumari," says Devon. "I *really* thought everyone knew by now. I mean, even Janine and Shejal just figured it out. So I thought Kumari did too. Bleddy hell, everyone bleddy-well knew before *I* did."

"Everyone except Kumari, shame."

Neha glances at the leftovers of the feast. "So, just us, huh?"

"Ah, come here," says Devon as he draws her into a hug. "Is res still so lonely?"

"Oh, it's okay, I feel a bit lost now and then, but its fine, nothing I can't handle. You know," she says, changing tone, "it's so weird, there aren't any other Indian people in my classes … none of them are doing BAs, brah!"

Devon sits back for what promises to be one of Neha's amusing stories as her animated eyes grow wider. "I'm serious, it's just me in between a few black kids who look at me suspiciously, and then the majority are whiteys. And it's so funny, they all have storybook names."

Devon laughs at her odd observations.

"For *real*, brah, they all have names like Anne and Julian and Dick and George and Tim; like characters from a book. I half expected some-one to stand up and say, I'm Jane Eyre, or something like that."

"Shame," says Devon, "we can ask Ahmed Essop to write a book about Neha Daya."

"Oh ja, very funny, I want to see if *that* sells."

Janine and Shejal flit towards the front door, Shejal waving a sheep-ish goodbye as he passes.

"Bye Pop, see you on campus!" shouts Neha.

"It's really nice having her here," says Devon as they hear Janine talking quietly on the front step. "The house feels less like a morgue."

"Some people are so weird," says Neha. "I still can't believe that her parents were demanding money from her."

"I know, it's crazy, especially since she's amazing, that girl … She does almost everything around the house." Then, as Janine enters, he says, "Finally! I have my wife back."

Neha smiles pleasantly at Devon's charity case, hiding her surprise at how close they have become.

✳

The Oriental Plaza in Fordsburg stands on the corner of 6th Avenue and Lilian Street; a collection of small shops lining the myriad arcades, crammed passages and basements of an old and weathered brown building. Devon views it as a mammoth. A giant creature hidden behind a huge coat that protects it against the harsh environment – just as this building once protected the old Indian shopkeepers for whom it became a space where they were allowed to trade to the public. A space away from the grander metropolis of Johannesburg and the pristine white suburbs in which their presence would have been aesthetically unpleasing, threatening and downright illegal. Even now, everything about the Plaza speaks of hiding, for how can these tiny rundown shops be viewed as economically threatening? The bland brick face conceals all the colourful treasures of the Orient with a heavy-handed modesty. Despite its roaring trade, the Plaza has not once been revamped since it was built in the 70s. Like a mammoth, it belongs to a bygone era. This is why Devon thinks that in order for the Plaza to survive, a necessary evolution is in the offing. And soon after taking over the shop, he starts renovating his store, much to the annoyance of the other shopkeepers.

"Won't you get this wood out the walkway," says Mr Ameen as Devon opens the doors of the Brass and Glass Store.

"Good morning, Uncle," says Devon. "As soon as the workers come, I'll get them to move it."

He walks into the store and can still smell the glue and hot sawdust of change. He has stripped the floor and put sparkling white Italian tiles in place of the cracking linoleum. All of the old counters and shelves have been ripped out, the walls re-plastered and painted in a brilliant white. He smiles at the naked infancy of his renovations – he is creating a heaven of some kind. Today the new store front will be redone in clear glass and stand like an open and fresh face to the world. He smiles as he pictures the neat and fluid space of the Brass and Glass Store. None of those cluttered display windows like all the other shops.

"Morning, my boy," says Mr Munshi, making his regular morning rounds.

"Ah, morning, Uncle," says Devon, wiping his hands on his jeans before he sticks out his hand. Mr Munshi wears a pale blue cotton kurta and a beige topi. He leans firmly on his smooth wooden walking stick as he stretches for the handshake. He has the large white beard of Muslim piety, but Devon thinks he looks more like Father Time.

"Still busy with the shop, hey?"

"Yes, but it should be done by next week."

Despite his rambling sermons about business ethics, Devon is rather fond of Mr Munshi. He started the Curtain Boutique when the doors of the Plaza first opened. He is one of the Plaza veterans who work on their feet every single day. His sons have long since taken over the shop, but Mr Munshi, now retired, still comes to the Plaza each day, calling it his livelihood, his life. He walks around, because he does not know how to sit, and chats to the entire community of shopkeepers to pass the time.

"I don't know why you going through all this trouble," he says. "Your father traded in that shop for fifteen years with no problems."

Devon smiles tightly. None of them understand his desire to renovate. To them he is nothing more than a rookie with a lot to learn.

"People don't come to the Plaza to shop in nice shops, my boy," he continues. "People come to the Plaza for the personal customer service, for quality products at discounted prices. We offer value and quality in the product, not in the design of the shop." He pauses for breath. "It's like putting on make-up … Allah! What a sin, this kind of vanity. Let your heart be pure, let your heart be pure, my boy." Then strolls away, his slippers dragging on the floor as he moves along.

Devon thinks he sees the sad eyes of the mammoth in him.

❋

Janine scans through a bill for R 6 802, 20, all for Chinese plastic dolls. The cashier aisles are empty and she sees an opportunity for a break.

"Oh, you taking a smoke break?" asks Suleka, who sits at the till next to hers. "I'll join you."

"Do you mind if I make myself a cup of tea first?" asks Janine.

"Go ahead, girl, don't let Suleka stop you." She flicks her long, bright pink fingernails.

Janine walks over to the kitchen, but feels those long nails prick into the back of her red overall.

"Where are you going?"

"To the kitchen, I just told you."

"The kitchen is *that* way, girl." She sticks out her extended index finger in the opposite direction.

"No, it's *not*," says Janine laughing. "I didn't start working here yesterday."

"Well, it looks like you have, girl," says Suleka, using her flat coloured intonations to stress her correctness. She pulls Janine by pinching her overall between her thumb and forefinger and leads her to another room.

Janine stares in amazement at what unfolds before her. "Oh my hell."

"Ja, I told you, it's kak lekker, neh?"

"I was using the kitchen and the toilet on the other side all this time. Oh my God, you have a microwave in here!" She runs into the adjacent bathroom. "There's even toilet paper!"

Her excitement deflates as she stares at the delicate peach finishing on the curtains. No one told her about this bathroom and kitchen. No one saved her from the gag reflex of the other side.

"Ja, jy sien … the other day I saw you walking into that vrot bathroom and that's when I thought, no man, Suleka will be your saviour."

And indeed, Janine does feel as if she has crossed over into heaven, having suffered so many months in that purgatorial bathroom and kitchen.

"Thank you, Suleka."

"Suleka got your back, girl," she says, sticking out her hands like a gangster. "Now don't go back into the black peoples' toilet, neh."

"What?"

"Ja, this is for the white workers and that one is for the black workers."

"But we're not white, brah."

"But we not black, brah." She flicks her neck from side to side. "And like heellloo," she makes circles in the air with her finger, "apartheid ended, like ... some time ago."

"So why the hell is there still a black peoples' toilet and why does it still look like kak?"

"It's not a racialist thing, it's a matter of job class," says Suleka, speaking slowly to explain. "See, we are cashiers and that is not the same as the black people who are the parcel packers and box carriers and drivers and whatever else they do."

"Ja, but we're not managers and clerks and accountants." She thinks through all of the positions that white people hold in the store.

"Ja, but ... see, here's the thing ..." says Suleka with her hands on her hips, "some years ago the floor manager said that I could use this toilet cos she could only just imagine how filthy the other one is. It's not that they racialist, Janine, I mean, I understand. It's cos black people, they can't look after their shit man. If you let them use the same toilet then they just going to make *this* one look like *that* one! Black people don't know how to look after their shit – Indians and coloured people at least have *some* pride."

"I thought they treated us all like kak, but turns out ..."

"Eish, are we still going for a smoke or what?"

"Ja, of course," says Janine, needing it now more than ever.

※

80

"Oh God, Shejal," says Neha, having watched him in the distance flirting with a group of frivolous girls. "You really have to get rid of those irritating chicks. Just let them know you're in a serious relationship already!"

"Oh, it's hardly as serious as you make it sound. What do you expect? That Janine and I will get married someday, have a few kids?"

"Why not?" asks Neha, though she already knows his reasons.

"Really, Neha! I already abandoned their little shop; can you imagine if I ever took Janine home? I will be cast out by my family forever." His head drops between his knees.

"The cost of freedom is high, my friend. Didn't Mandela teach you anything? Twenty-seven years of banishment. That's the irony of freedom, Shej, it's hardly ever for free—" She stops short, feeling her father's words popping out of her mouth.

"Neha!" yells a voice from afar.

She rolls her eyes and keeps her back still in the hope that she will turn into a plant.

"Oohwee," says Shejal gleefully, "does Neha have a boyfriend?"

"Shut the fuck up," she mutters, turning to face the inevitable. "Hi, Govind, how you doing?"

"Oh, I'm cool, man."

Shejal snorts and tries to stifle the rest of his laugh.

"Just came back to res hoping to have some lunch." Govind pauses. "So, did you manage to organise me some fresh chow?"

"Yes, I have like a whole twenty lunch tins' worth of food," says Neha. "I'll go get them."

"Ey," says Govind once Neha is gone, "are you Neha's stekkie?"

Shejal can only shake his head. The Durban accent proves to be more than his Lenz sensibilities can handle.

"So, what you studying, ey?" asks Govind.

"Comp sci. You?"

"I'm doing aeronautical engineering." He puffs out his chest.

"So you from … Durban?"

"Yes, I'm from Umhlanga North."

He says it proudly, but Shejal is unsure what there is to be proud of; he would hate to be from *anywhere* in Durban.

"Oh Neha," says Govind once she returns with food in tow. He peers inside the lunch tins to see what her mother has prepared this week. "Oh man, dhol! I love your mother's dhol." He beams like a child. "Just let me take these containers up and then I'll bring the money down now-now."

"Ey, Neha, your mother's dhol," quips Shejal as soon as Govind has left.

He and Neha roll on the grass in an act of purgation, letting out a deluge of laughter.

"Eish, that Govind. I met him in the first week and he has been on my tail ever since."

"So, what, he asked you to go out with him?"

"No, I dunno, he's a bit creepy. At first I thought he was so clingy cos he's homesick and I'm the only Indian in my res, so I'm like the natural option for him, you know, to talk to. But then he started giving me these lines about how us Indians must stick together." She winces. "I mean, what the hell does that mean? *Us* Indians must stick together?" She thinks of, and approves of, the kind of scolding her father would give a boy like this.

"What the hell are you people doing?" asks Kumari, seeing their flushed faces.

"Oh, just spying on Neha's boyfriend," says Shejal

"You have a boyfriend?" shouts Kumari, not sure how many of these revelations she can take.

"No, he's talking shit."

"Wait, wait, he's coming back, you must see him, man, one handsome *fella* she found, ey? Sit, sit … here's he coming."

"There you go," says Govind as he hands Neha some folded notes. "It's sixty rands, I hope that's enough."

"Sure, thanks."

"Hi, I'm Govind," he says as he spots the new face.

"Oh hi, I'm Kumari," she responds shyly.

"Oh really?" he laughs. "That's my mother's name."

Kumari blushes lightly, smiling after Govind as he heads back to res.

"And you accuse me of being a greedy capitalist?" snorts Shejal.

"He insisted on paying, so what could I do?" Neha says. "Besides, my mother shouldn't have to slave away in the kitchen for free. He *should* pay, don't you think?"

"You sell your mother's food to him?" asks Kumari. "Shame, why are you exploiting the poor boy? It can't be easy being so far away from home." Her heart is full of sympathy for this handsome stranger.

September 1995

"How lucky that we are five," shouts Kumari over the music. "Just enough to fill the car! Gosh, remember how we used to dream about taking all those trips out of Lenz when we were kids?"

Shejal zips down the M1N highway in a car that he can finally call his own. He is treating his friends to a night out on the town. "Can you feel the acceleration on this baby?" he asks, pressing down on the pedal.

They fly along in the little black capsule towards their next adventure, Shejal concentrating his efforts on breaking the 120km/hr speed limit. The world begins to brush past them as the momentum of the car makes long straight strokes across the neat face of the world, smudging it into a soft palette of colour and light, breaking the hard lines of rectangles set in concrete and glass into twirls and curls without distinction. The streetlights ripple in the car with shutter-speed frenzy as their bodies push further into the cushioned seats. The tyres blend into one indistinguishable swoosh of sound as they fly, fly forward.

Janine turns and smiles at Shejal, so pleased with himself and his new toy. His hands loosely caress the steering wheel as he tries to turn driving into an art form of its own. Janine can almost see him sitting on the floor as a 5-year old playing with his plastic cars and making vroom-vroom noises.

"Seriously, Shej," says Neha, "you really are a spoilt brat."

Shejal laughs. The long wait proved worth it. His father has more than just delivered, he is now the proud owner of the new E Class E320 and finds no easy way to dispute Neha's claim.

"Oh look," shouts Neha, "my dear, dear university!"

The orange streetlights that dot the highway tint their faces with warm sunset shades. They all crane their necks to the right as a mountain of naked concrete rises up in front of them.

"Looks like a jail," says Devon.

They make their way past the bouncers, who stand at the entrance like broad sturdy doors, and enter the hot, dark chaos of the club. Shejal heads straight to the bar, determined to get drunk and sober quicker than the rest of them so that he can drive home. Janine, Devon, Kumari and Neha wait in the corner, standing on the outskirts of the throbbing crowd.

Shejal comes back with a half-spilt drink in his hand. "Joh, I had to fight off all the ouens just to get this," he shouts as he brushes the spillage off his shirt.

"Oh my God," says a shrill voice from behind and he feels a hand tighten around his wrist. "Shejal, is that you?"

"Oh hi," says Shejal tentatively to this girl who has still not let go of his arm.

"Kajal," she says, spotting his discomfort.

"Oh yes, that's right, I met you before … on campus."

"Yes," she shouts, enthusiastically drunk, "and you know Deepa, right?" Kajal yanks her friend around the waist and loops her into the conversation. "Shejal, Deepa. Deepa, Shejal." She steps back to bring them close enough to shake hands.

Deepa stretches her arm forward. "It's a pleasure." She tucks a stray piece of hair behind her ear and smiles shyly; her dimples dazzle in the dim light.

"You know Neha and Kumari, right?" asks Shejal in an effort to get Kajal to let go of his arm.

"Oh yes, of course," says Kajal and offers them a remote smile. "So, aren't you going to dance?"

"No, not yet." He looks at his friends. Most of them are rolling their eyes at his obnoxious acquaintance.

"Oh, come on, man," says Kajal as she yanks him by the arm again.

Shejal stretches his other arm out to Janine and she catches the drink that dangles from his hand.

"I'll hold it for you," she says, watching him disappear into the throb of dancers with Kajal ushering him through, using her hips to part the sea of people. Janine feels a burn build around her temples and she touches them with the side of the plastic cup; condensation runs down the sides of her face. She catches glimpses of him; his wide smile, his laugh, his arms reaching out with ease, pulling someone to dance with him. This dissected rendition of minute betrayal flashes in hideous neon green and hot ultra-violet. How he loves the adoration; abandoning her in favour of the crowd, playing to these girls with laboriously painted make-up, blow-dried hair, expensive clothes and a higher education. She shrinks into the corner as she rubs the trim of her synthetic cotton T-shirt from Mr Price. She drains the plastic cup down to the last drop, crushes it in her hand and tosses it on the ground, feeling her own disposability.

Kumari fans herself as she breathes out loudly. "I'm sweating."

"Aren't we all?" Neha asks, offering her a serviette.

"No man, my hair," she says, running her hands over her ponytail. "It's gonna go kroes in here. It's so not fair. I spent two hours trying to get it straight."

"Come on," says Devon, "this is too much faffing. Let's go dance already."

He drags them to the floor, mostly in an effort to distract Janine from the bad mood that is brewing, and it is not long before they are smiling again, laughing at each other's less than perfect form.

Soon a pair of arms folds around Neha's waist and hoists her into the air. She watches her friends' faces from high as they stand still in surprise.

"Govind!" says Kumari as she smoothes down her hair. "Oh my God … What are you doing here?"

"You then told me about the party here?" says Govind, utterly confused.

Neha glares at Kumari and storms off with Janine and Devon in tow. Kumari turns to follow, but Govind gets her to dance with him instead.

"You okay?" asks Devon as he watches Janine burn her way through her third consecutive cigarette.

"Ja, ja," comes her too-quick reply between greedy sucks on a burnt-out butt.

Devon looks around at the faces in the club. All of them seem to be etched in different shades of hunger; everywhere he looks he sees someone trying too hard, drinking too much, smoking too heavily and shouting too loudly. His heart sinks at what turns out to be less than the adventure he expected – a trip for desperate souls.

As he walks into the shop, Devon feels a sense of great satisfaction. These first months have been arduous ones, learning about import laws and restrictions, about balancing the books and taxation, about maintaining a store and dealing with the clientele. He marvels at his ability to succeed at something he has no natural interest in whatsoever, but he could not let the shop go, not after losing both his parents – this is the only legacy he has left.

He switches on the subtle backlights and the empty glass vases begin to glow as they bend the light around their smooth curves. Being in the shop is like having a conversation with his dead father. It is as if he is now answering the eternal question of "How was your day, Dad?" For Devon begins to see exactly what his father's life must have been like, sitting amongst the quiet glory of these shining tombs of light.

He lifts his eyes from the page as customers walk in, nods politely and returns to the book that he pretends to be reading to give the couple a chance to browse in peace. Other shop owners use subtle tactics to discourage customers from "just looking". The Oriental Plaza is not a browsers' market but a buyers' market and very few people still appreciate this style of shopping. The interactive sport of bargaining is becoming extinct now that the fixed prices of the leisurely malls do not require people to break a sweat. Having adopted a calmer strategy, Devon imagines how his customers must enjoy roaming through his shop, feeling relaxed that he does not pester them to buy something.

"Eh, excuse me," says the lady.

"Yes?"

"Well, these vases, we need about fifty – we're wedding decorators."

"How much if we take fifty?" asks the man, not mincing his words.

Devon walks over and examines the price card that sits just below the vase.

"It's one hundred and sixty rands for one," he says, "so for fifty, it would cost…" He calculates. "Eight thousand."

"Yes, but what's the special price?" asks the man impatiently.

"Oh, that is the first and final price. We don't bargain in the Brass and Glass Store," says Devon with a smile. "It's a more liberal approach; everyone pays the same price and no one feels cheated."

"But the man who runs this store, he always gives us a discount for buying in bulk. That's why we came back," says the lady.

"Oh, my father, he passed away last year," says Devon, mildly annoyed at the frequency with which this comes up.

"He used to give us great discounts," says the lady.

"Ja, and he was a lot more helpful too," says the man.

"Well, I'm sorry you feel that way. If you like the vase, take it. If you are unwilling to pay for it, then leave it. I'm the sole importer for that Spanish cut of glass in this area, so you are welcome to try and find it at a better price."

The couple frowns at him.

"I'm not going to grovel, like you expect all of us Indian shopkeepers to do," he continues, imagining his father licking the boots of these two insidious wedding decorators.

"Well, I think we're done here," says the man, and the couple storms out of the shop.

Devon spots Mr Munshi watching him through the clear glass front. For the first time, he regrets putting it in. The drama in his shop is now a public affair.

The old man comes in and shakes his head in disappointment.

"Things have changed, times have changed and yet we still trading like we at the mercy of these customers. We setting the bar really low for ourselves," says Devon, but Mr Munshi just continues to shake his head. "We not so hungry anymore. We should stop acting like it. Don't we have any pride?" he continues.

"Who do you think your father was, my boy, Harry Oppenheimer? You doing a great dishonour to his memory by spitting on his life's work like this," the old man says before he leaves.

※

Shejal drives Deepa home. She approached him at university earlier in the day, inviting him out for lunch. He hadn't been able to say no to her dimples and her grey eyes shining like hot, silver amulets.

Those same amulets are looking at him now. "I was always left guessing if you liked me or not," she remarks coyly.

"Oh, I'm just a coward, I guess."

He takes the off-ramp into Lenasia, his hands turn the steering wheel with pre-calculated force. As he drives, thick black smoke from a nearby veld fire covers them. The car passes through the pocket of heat and Shejal's conscience begins to burn with a strength that he has not yet anticipated. It catches him off guard and he begins to rattle in the cushioned folds of his seat. Every single street bears an inscription of Janine; the tiny house-shop on Rose Avenue, the swings in the park, every single corner on Willow Street brings her to mind. Her smiles, her sadness, her hot temper and the fiery touches of her hands are as entangled as the weeds.

After dropping Deepa at home, he has the coldest of showers and changes his clothes before he gorges on a plate of his mother's food. She has started cooking good meals again, which he reads as a sign that she is finally coming to terms with the pre-election, election and post-election jitters. He goes to his room to clear his head, but Heema barges in.

"Don't you know how to knock?"

"Oh my God," she whispers, although he can tell that she wants to scream instead. "I can't believe you took the bait."

"What the hell are you talking about?"

"About Deepa!"

Shejal jerks off his chair.

"I would never have thought, in a *million* years, that you, of all people, *you*, would take the bait and actually fall for a girl our grandmother chose."

"Oh my God." He tries to figure out the plot and then digest the story. His tongue begins to thicken in his mouth and a bitter taste rises to his throat. "But I met her in a club and at Wits."

She smiles pitifully at him. "It's actually quite clever, neh? Kajal, who happens to be Nalini Kaki's Masi's daughter, yep, she's family of some kind, suggested that you two should be introduced in a less obvious way after Maa chose this hand-picked Prajapati girl for her favourite grandson. They were just trying to speak your language, I guess. You know, meet you where you at, kinda thing."

"Why didn't you tell me?"

"Hell, I thought you were so stuck on that dark chick of yours, just so you can piss them off, but here you are giving them a reason to celebrate."

"Shut the fuck up, Heem."

"Sjoe, I was rather waiting for the whole plot to blow up in their faces, but joh, Maa is actually making sweet rice in the kitchen."

Shejal stands still. His eyes stare stonily at the floor. The only signs of movement are the feverish shades of red that dance across his face.

Later he goes to the kitchen, to taint their sweet rice with his gall.

Devon stares into the still flame of the candle, struggling to clear his mind during his prayer session. What? he asks silently, finally submitting to the vision that has only grown more intense with time. The water cascades in veils in front of him, as if he is on the inside of a waterfall. The pressure of the fall keeps his body still, the enormous strength blocking him from what lies beyond. Still, in his mind's eye, he tries to pierce this veil and, in an instant, the waters stop. His heart slows down and his weight becomes soft again. A field of green extends before him with a moody sun above. There is the sound of benign thunder in the distance. Then a young man appears. He walks across the field and plays a harmonica. Devon tries to get closer to this figure – perhaps this is someone he recognises – but as he sets his concentration, his body tenses and the image fades.

He gets up in frustration. Still, the memory of the man lingers, and he feels a loneliness he has never felt before. He seeks out Janine's company, finding her in the kitchen, preparing supper.

"You left the door open again," she says. "Ja, ja, I was watching, but just for a little bit." She shows him a centimetre between her two fingers. "It looks like a nice thing to do or a nice place to be."

"It's not time travel. But ja, sometimes you feel and see the most amazing things," he says wistfully, watching her drain pasta in the sink.

"Oooh, like what?"

"Well, today I kept seeing lots and lots of water falling in front of me, like I was inside a waterfall or a rain cloud or something – what?" he asks, seeing her snigger.

"Nothing, carry on … lots and lots of water."

"So anyways, then the water just fell away and I saw this man—"

Janine breaks out into a snort.

"What? Just tell me."

"It's nothing, really," she says, trying to control herself. "It's just that my friend, Suleka, from work, she told me that whenever she dreams of water, she knows she is sexually frustrated."

"It's not porn, it's a prayer."

"But come on, brah, you saw a man as well. Hectic!"

"Did it ever occur to you that it could have been Jesus Christ, you dirty beast?"

"Hey, I just told you what I heard," says Janine with a shrug.

November 1995

"It will hold," says Janine, looking up at the sky, adamant that their Sunday picnic plan will not be cancelled due to rain.

"Ja, we can't cancel," says Neha, "this is Devon's big gay day."

Shejal walks away from the girlish banter to wait in the car. He prefers to keep the idea of his gay friend in the closet of his mind.

"Ja, come let's go," says Kumari. "Govind will be waiting."

"Hey, that boyfriend of yours can wait a little longer," says Neha, still wavering on whether to load the large umbrella in the boot.

"Can you all just get the fuck in the car!" shouts Shejal who already has the engine idling.

"Take it easy, Shej," says Kumari.

"Ja, chillax." Janine puts out her hand to soothe this restless anger that has been stirring for weeks now. He flinches at her touch. He pulls his hand away from the gear and leaves her fingers trailing mid-air.

"I still can't believe I let you talk me into a blind date," says Devon.

"Relax, brah. I told you already, I just said some friends are having a picnic and that he should come. So if you hit it off, that's great," says Neha.

Janine watches Shejal grind his teeth, trying to block out the conversation. Something has happened. They rarely ever laugh together anymore and sex comes in uncomfortable staccatos which are now followed by audible silences. The small gap between their seats seems like a cruel joke. She wonders how he always manages to do this to her, slowly coaxing her to open her heart and then slamming a door on it without any explanations.

As they drive through Johannesburg's green suburbs, the soft trees with generous arms bow over the streets and cover them like an umbrella. The stoic jacarandas bear silent witness, weeping their purple blooms.

"Ey man, pizza is getting cold," says Govind when they meet him on the lawn at Zoo Lake.

"We should wait for David," says Neha half-heartedly, but everyone has already dug in.

"Who's David?" asks Govind.

"You know, David, he stays in your res."

"Aiyoo, Ram Ram …" he says to cleanse himself. "That David – why you invited him? Everyone says he's a full-time moffie. What? I'm not joking. Ryan, that boy who stays next to him told me. So, I keep far away from him!"

"Oh shit…" says Janine as they hear a crack of thunder.

"No, no, no," Neha begs the greying skies. "David hasn't come yet."

"See, it's a sign," says Govind. "Why you inviting moffies to hang around with us?"

"The same reason we inviting Durbanites to hang with us," Neha mutters under her breath.

"Okay, time to move," says Kumari as she wipes a raindrop from her face. "Come on, everyone in Govind's car, it's bigger."

Just as they all stuff themselves in, the rain begins to pelt down and the roof turns into a harsh tinny drum. It is so loud that they cannot hear each other or the radio. Within a few minutes it begins to grow hot and the windows are misty.

"Eish, turn on the air conditioner, brah," says Shejal.

"No ways, it wastes petrol."

Neha begins to doodle in the mist on the window, and on the other side Devon places his head against the cold glass for relief.

"Don't do that," says Janine as she slaps him on the hand, "you're going to mess up your hair."

"So what? It doesn't matter anymore."

"Hey, look … tha-wha! Rain's stopping," says Govind with childish delight.

Everyone gives an audible sigh of relief as the storm is replaced by the gentlest of drizzles.

Devon stares out, watching the last of the rain run down the window. The drops collect, forming streams and rivers that all roll down the pane. He rubs the sheet of mist away with his palm and the world outside reappears. He can already see someone on the lawns; a solitary figure in the distance, frivolously kicking up the dew with private joy. As the person comes closer, Devon rolls down his window in disbelief: a man with a harmonica! "Jesus Christ," he whispers to himself.

"Oh my sack, it's David! He's still come!" Neha jumps out of the car to meet him.

Devon tries to follow, but his legs have turned to jelly. The last drops of water shake off the car door and he wakes from reality to his dream.

Neha flags Devon over with her hands. He swabs his clammy palms on his jeans. This is the part of the vision that he does not know – the end. He musters up the courage to step in, to become a player and participate.

"Smell that freshness, hey?" says David. He wipes his harmonica on his cargo shorts and slips it in his pocket.

"You play the harmonica?" asks Devon, trying to hide the residual sense of awe.

"Oh yeah," he chuckles, "it's something I picked up while travelling through Europe last year during the holidays. I used to carry it with me all the time and now it's like a bad habit that I can't break. I know, I know … it's very boho," he says self-consciously. "Ah, look, they've opened up the boating again. We should go out on the lake …"

"I don't know how to row," says Devon.

"Ah, come on, it will be great. It's so easy. Come, come, the others will catch up."

"You two go ahead without me," says Neha, bowing out coyly.

But Kumari, once she sees where they are heading, drags Govind after them. This is romance, she thinks, the two of them out on the solitary lake together.

"There you go." David gives Kumari and Govind a push out of the small dock and sends their little boat circling in the water.

Devon's trip starts on a calmer note. He is in good hands. David rows out and on, effortlessly.

"Oh, this is sweet, bru," says David as he glances across the glittering body of water. "Can you hear that? It's a sacred ibis." He points towards the cluster of trees that grows on the island in the middle of the lake.

"You like birds?"

"Well, my father used to take us birdwatching when we were kids, so it's just some leftover useless information … Your friends seem to be having fun," he laughs.

Devon turns in his seat to watch Govind and Kumari spin around in circles, not far from where they started. In comparison, David makes broad strokes as he cuts through the water. He leans his back forward in perfect intervals and Devon can smell his musky aftershave and the faint veil of sweat that has broken out on his skin.

"Sjoe," he sighs, putting the oars to rest in their locks. "Do you mind if we just leave it here for a while? Have to save some of my strength for rowing back."

Devon does not answer, still too stunned. David might dissolve into an insubstantial stream of air if he speaks back to him, this mirage. He cannot help but stare; the two plank seats are parallel to one another, putting him and David in each other's direct line of sight.

"You don't talk much, hey?" asks David with a smile. "Neha told me a lot about you. Are you guys best friends?"

"Ja, you could call us that."

"Devon," says David, trying out the name on his tongue. "What does that mean?"

"Not sure, guess my mother just liked it. And you're David, like the king."

"Yes, exactly that. So very Jewish of my mother, huh?"

"Oh wow, you're a Jew?'

"Well, as Jewish as a gay man is allowed to be and wants to be, I guess. I pitch up for the big occasions, you know, but otherwise I can't be bothered much … You know, until Neha, I'd never met a Hindu before. And," he pauses, "I never met a gay Hindu before – so it's a first."

Devon laughs heartily before he replies, "I'm not a Hindu, I'm actually a Christian. An Anglican," he adds quickly; this distinction is important to him. "Neha didn't tell me that she told you that I am …"

"No, she didn't. It's my sixth sense! It's never let me down, years of practice. So, you are gay, right?"

"Ja, I guess."

"You guess?"

"Well, I've never, you know …" He starts to wriggle on the hard wooden seat as the boat begins to grow small.

"You're kidding. Not a *single* time?"

"No, never."

"So you've just been with girls all this time?"

"No, not even that," says Devon with a laugh, feeling ridiculous.

"Wow." David's eyebrows make a visible leap. "This *is* a first, for sure. All the gay men I've met are all raging whores! Myself included." The boat rocks gently with his laughter.

"Oh Govind, just give me the damn oars," says Kumari with growing irritation.

"Just sit back, woman."

They move in circles again as Govind shifts the water beneath them.

"We haven't even moved away from the dock," says Kumari, pointing towards it in embarrassment. "Give them here," she mutters as she snatches them from him and begins to row. The boat slowly begins to back away from the dock and she sees the boat tenders and onlookers clap mockingly.

Once they have moved further into the middle of the lake, she drops her arms limply. Govind pulls the oars away from her again. "Let me do it," he says through stiff lips.

"Fine, just don't make me too dizzy this time." She folds her arms and sits firmly on her plank as she watches his muscles bulge from the strain of his furious and futile rowing. "Well, sorry for trying to teach you something," she snaps.

"I don't need you to teach me anything," says Govind, glaring at her.

As soon as the picnic is set out Neha goes off by herself, leaving Janine to sit with Shejal whose unbearable silence eventually pushes her towards a desperate confession. "You know … I *do* love you, Shej." The words, like prisoners, break out of their ancient shackles.

"Is this what this is to you?" he asks dryly. She sees his Adam's apple bounce in alarm and the gates roll over his eyes again. "Is that what you want?"

She feels old shame, the kind her father made her feel, of wanting to say "yes" to such a question.

He dusts off his jeans and starts to pace about.

"Well… what does this mean to you?" she asks coolly, laying herself flat and rational, cold and steely, like an operating table upon which he endlessly examines himself.

"I don't know. I don't know. I don't know what I'm doing or where I'll end up, and there's just so much more to life," he says as he shakes his head. "I hate picnics, I hate them so much" he mutters.

She shivers. She knows exactly what he means. And why.

"I have to go," he says.

Neha sits alone on the bench beside the lake and watches ducklings wade against the unexpected force of an undercurrent. Their mother soon comes to help buck the tide and Neha warms at the sight of her gentle propulsion. She too relates to this maternal pride as she thinks of her friends, all settled into their pairs because of her: Janine and Shejal have her to thank for forcing them to finally take their relationship to a new level, Kumari and Govind would never have met without her, and now there are Devon and David, who seem to be hitting it off. Like a god, she remains seated at her remote vantage point, musing over her masterful designs when Shejal plants himself next to her on the bench. "Remember Suicide Valley?"

His question is too abrupt, unexpected. It chases away all this love that has flourished under her watch. She throws a limp slice of pizza into the lake and watches the ducks flock to fight for it amongst themselves. Their thunderous quacks make it impossible to speak, but when they leave just as suddenly, the silence shrouds her in shame.

"There was nothing we could do," she says.

"Nothing. No."

They stare ahead, thinking of ghosts they wish they could forget.

September 1996

Already drenched from the rain, Janine waits patiently on the side of the road, hoping that an empty taxi will drive past. She watches the people, as she always does, going home from work in their comfortable cars. She brushes the wet strands of hair away from her face and sticks out her hand with new determination – her index finger pointing up; the CBD signal. She places her free hand on her hip, standing there like an aggressive hooker.

Finally, a taxi pulls up and the door rolls open. She waits for a young boy to jump out before she bends her head and crouches as she gets in, taking the only seat that is left. In accordance with taxi etiquette, it is her job to pull the door shut on its rolling wheels. A squeak, followed by a heavy thud is heard, the taxi shakes a little; all the signs and vibrations of a long life on the road. She tries to make herself more comfortable on her small seat by shifting her weight around, but it wobbles on its broken base and part of her bum is forced to rest on the thigh of the passenger to her right. After a while she feels her muscles strain; it is more like crouching in the air than sitting. The dampness from everyone's clothes multiplies along with the day's sweat, making the taxi an uncomfortable box to be in. She is relieved to announce her "Sho't left!" when her stop appears.

She strolls up Sauer Street and sees something romantic in the paved walkways and grand buildings even though they are glazed with years of smog and urine. The CBD is a Cinderella story in reverse – everyone who can afford to has left – but the city is far from orphaned. She enjoys weaving between the heart of the hustle: the toothless man and his muti, the fat ladies with babies tied to their backs selling fruits and vegetables, the flashy black boys hawking pantsula caps and fake branded clothing, the elderly man with the dubiously acquired jewellery, watches and sunglasses, the agents handing out pamphlets advertising for illegitimate doctors who guarantee miracles.

Janine passes the Johannesburg library with its broad steps, then turns right into Market Street. Plastic bags whisk about, crashing into people and buildings just like the storm that has recently passed through the city. She makes a game of catching each of the bags underfoot, but the wind sweeps them over and across her face again and she is delighted by her defeat as she finds herself spinning in a sea of colourful jellyfish. She makes a left turn into Loveday; the street is full of people eager to get back to Lenz. She joins them, waiting her turn to get into yet another taxi and go home.

David lounges on Devon's bed with his head resting on his arm. They have been together ever since their boat ride, but Devon still thinks that David belongs with someone who, like him, can devote their entire life to whimsical passions. *An animal rights activist or a novelist*, he thinks. David is heir to South Africa's largest plastic manufacturing company. After two years at business school, he quit to travel the world. He has no particular commitment to a career in anthropology either, but studies because it broadens his mind. While Devon has been keeping the shroud off his father's business, David has never been refused any adventure, and his enchantment lies in his ability to lay out a smorgasbord of cultural experiences in a single conversation. Today they are discussing his last trip to India, and on the subject of saris, Devon has begun searching for his mother's old collection to show to him.

"In India, it was so fascinating that women even wore saris when doing construction work," says David.

"Nope, that's not it," says Devon as he casts aside a stray piece of cloth. Then, glancing back at David, he says, "Look at you, sitting there like a fat queen."

"Shut up, if you didn't feed me so much, I wouldn't have this belly." He rubs his rounding stomach luxuriously. "But I do love me some curry."

Finally, Devon finds what he is looking for and empties the suitcase, sending the light material cascading across the room like party streamers. He drapes them over David's arms and chest.

"Oh man…" says David, sitting up to examine them.

Devon watches him run the fabric through his fingers as attentively as if he were spinning cotton.

"This is my first time," says David, throwing the excess cloth across his body with a dramatic swish.

Devon notices that this is David's favourite phrase around him, as if he were just another adventure to consume.

"So, mister, does it tickle your fancy?" David asks coyly from behind the impromptu veil he has made for himself.

Devon assents; he lets the fantasy play out by pulling him closer. David cannot take his eyes away from the enchanted hands that undress him; there is tremendous erotic power in watching himself being handled amidst the soft sheer fabric.

Neha nibbles on the small details of Frik's life like a curious rat. She pokes around his bathroom, noting the toothpaste squeezed at the top and left fat at the bottom, the mushy blue soap that floats in the dish, the toothbrush with splayed-out bristles and the towels that do not match. She loves unearthing these seemingly useless facts about people's lives, seeing them as indicative icebergs of hidden secrets and selves. Having Frik in her life has turned her into a certified snoop.

"You okay in there?" he asks from behind the door.

She hears him shift outside and she closes the cabinet as softly as she can. "Yup, I'll be out soon."

Frik just joined Wits University this year. After completing his BA, he taught First Language Afrikaans at a high school in Krugersdorp. One year at that job was enough to scare him out of the big bad world and back into his decision to do a master's degree in translation studies.

He plants a sudden kiss on her lips as she finally comes out of the bathroom. His arms around her small body prick her flesh, made numb from what feels like years of isolation.

"Neha," he says with a heavy emphasis on the 'h'. "I love saying your name."

"Frik," she says, feeling like she just bit into a piece of wood. "Me too," she giggles. In truth, she hates his name for all the images and cheap associations it conjures up in the back of her mind.

"Bon appetit," he says, pronouncing all the letters. He shows her the steaming bowls of two-minute noodles that lie waiting on the couch. "What?" he asks. "You're always laughing at me and making me feel like a doos."

"Nothing, it's just your accent. It's funny."

"Oh well, so is *yours*."

"No, it's not! English is my first language, okay."

"Okaey," he says, mimicking her flat 'a'.

"Shut up, man, you're bloody Afrikaans," she retorts, insulted that he is comparing their English proficiencies.

"And you're what? English?"

"It's complicated, you wouldn't understand."

"Oh, trust me, I get it, it's embarrassing to be who you really are."

"See, I told you, you don't get it. I am not a fucken Indian, if that's what you mean. I don't have a language except English and neither do my parents. Oh, but we were forced to learn Afrikaans." She waits for the sting to register on his face.

"I'm sick of this country where I have to treat my mother tongue like an albatross. Thank God, I'll be gone soon, as soon as I can help it."

An awkward silence develops between them, feeling ashamed about the blows that they have dealt each other. Amongst the flickering light-bulb, the tasteless two-minute noodles and the cobwebs, she finds ample reason to respect him, to love him.

"I'm sorry," she says, flying the dove from her side of the couch to his. "I admire how true to your roots you are."

"Fuck off. You think it's stupid, but its fine." He shrugs. "I can't change the past, you know."

"But then why live in it?"

"Huh?"

"I mean, can't we just acknowledge the respective contributions that our people have made in the past and move on?"

"Contributions. Ja, as if any of our ancestors had such pleasant mo-tives," he sniggers. "They were all motivated by money, yours and mine."

"So what then? I should learn Hindi and take a boat back to India?"

"If that floats your boat, why not? If you asking me to wear the flag on my back, you can forget it," he adds, used to her New South Africa sentiments.

"But you said you hated it yourself, that what you saw at that Afri-kaans school scared you, you said it yourself!" she shouts. "And how *dare* you expect me to embrace a culture that I never even had. Who's the fucken colonialist now? Who wants to keep the fucking Indian?"

This is how they choose to spend their time, undressing each other until they stand there, naked and raw, clinging together as they desperately search in one another for a new truth about themselves.

October 1996

Janine hears Shejal's laughter and is repulsed by its careless ring. She tries to keep herself away from this conversation that is centred on him as he narrates anecdotes about relatives from America who came to visit his family. She will not humour him in his desire to play the sun. It is an axis that she has broken away from and now she recklessly spins on her own orbit whose pattern and path is still ill-defined and vague to her. She mildly enjoys her adventure in the dark, her angry rebellion against his raging ego. But she runs out of tasks and succumbs to sitting down and listening – this story is clearly not going to end any time soon.

"The first night when they came over, they brought us a gift. It was, like, this big gift bag full of American sweets and chocolates and stuff. So that night, Jack threw a tantrum for the sweets and my mother opened it for him. And he ate the whole thing! It was so funny, joh … I could see my mother's eyeballs popping out of her head. That kid was just vreeting and vreeting, no shame."

"So they all like hectic fatties?" asks Devon.

"Well, Jack is as round as a ball, so ja …

Kumari rushes in gaily. "Sorry I'm late, people. I made dessert for us today."

"Can we eat now?" Janine whinges.

"Oh, but first a toast," announces Kumari theatrically while they all gather around the table. "To Neha and her boyfriend, Frik," she says, her glass lifted to the heavens.

Shejal spits his wine back into the glass as he laughs, but she adamantly stands her ground. "I'm serious!"

"About which part?" asks Janine. "Neha having a boyfriend, haha, or Neha having a boyfriend named Frik, haha-haha?"

"So nobody knows except me?" Kumari asks, looking at Neha. "Our little queen of secrets, huh?"

With her eyes as big as saucers, Neha flicks her head in confusion.

"Just sit down and eat," says Shejal.

"Well, Govind told me all about it. Ja, he knows too," she says coldly.

A piece of macaroni falls from Neha's lip. This is going to end badly.

"Govind saw you and him, *Frik*, and he cornered him on campus to find out what's his business with you," says Kumari trying to buy over her audience with this fact.

"Oh, that fucken Govind," screams Neha. "Why can't he mind his own business?" "What?" asks Janine. "So...it's for *real*?"

"You have a boyfriend and his name is Frik?" asks Shejal.

"That Govind, he's like fucken Frankenstein's monster," yells Neha, "following me around like that!"

"You know, Govind was just looking out for you, like a big brother would. You never know if you can trust people, even if he *is* a whitey."

Neha looks at her friends, all of whom wear smirks on their faces, their lips itching to say "Frik" over and over again. None of them will help her fight her war.

"You people are such sick snobs. You don't even know him. So what if he's Afrikaans?"

"At least you know how it feels," says Kumari. "Oh, Miss High-and-Mighty who wants to make fun of other people's boyfriends."

"So does he like sokkie-sokkie and stuff?" asks Janine, grinning.

"And does he play goeie rugby?" asks Shejal. "Come on, Neha, you say we don't know the guy, help us out here, does he wear shoes?"

Neha holds an angry silence as she sulks in front of them. When her relationship with Frik started it was a wonderful secret that was finally all hers. With time, she convinced herself that she was keeping the mystery of her private adventure alive by not sharing it with anyone. But now that it is out in the open, she knows that this is what she has been avoiding; this sense of shame that is being made hers to bear alone.

"You should bring him home," says Devon lightly. "I'm sure he's wonderful."

But Neha is in no mood for his appeasements. "This mac and cheese tastes like shit."

"You're being quiet and weird," says Frik.

She has been avoiding the gushy look on his face all afternoon, finding it quite intolerable. But he persists, watching her in profile as she bends over a book with her feet crossed on his couch.

"Have an assignment to finish, can't chat today, man," she says without looking up.

"Or you're anxious about being with me … because…" he says lightly, waiting for her to fill in the blank.

She whips her head to the side like a dog cocking its ears towards an interesting pitch. Frik is the only man that she has met who can call out her nonchalance. He is both smart and sensitive enough to see her even when she is in hiding.

"Would you ever introduce me to your people?" she asks.

"Well, would you like me to?" He is hesitant, then laughs. "Gosh, that would be one helluva dinner! And then you will wish I'd kept you in the dark instead."

"So you wouldn't, right?" she laughs too, feeling less like a racist for thinking the same.

"No," he says tentatively, "not if I can save us from that, no… What a useless waste of energy trying to cure everyone of their ignorance."

Perfectly put, "their ignorance", she thinks, then laughs again. She drops her pen, sighs with relief and moves the file that rests on her lap. "Ah, Frikkus."

She looks around at the dirty walls which crack and flake in the corners. She hears the footsteps of someone in the flat above and the grinding of the pipes as they turn on the taps. This little apartment of Frik's serves their purposes well, for they are apart from the world in this obscure block of flats in an even more obscure part of Braamfontein – cut off from space and time. She laughs with delight as she hears the bustling city life outside the building; the taxis hoot, the vendors call, the pigeons coo. Life passes by without glancing at them where they make love underneath the cool, mildewing ceiling.

"You're beautiful," he says.

Her eyes grow big with self-consciousness under his scrutinising gaze. All the scars from her childhood, spent in tomboy antics, sit like shadows on her face. She should have saved herself – for beauty – to be able to receive these words without trepidation. She looks at his scrawny face; his small, beady eyes and ruddy complexion with acne scars along his jawline. "You too, you're beautiful!" she sings, awakened to some as yet unknown generosity that bursts from her soul.

✳

After scouring all of the job ads in the classifieds of *The Star*, Janine finally finds the sign that she has been looking for: "No prior experience required. A starting position with potential for steady promotion (progress based)". Two days later she is on her way to the interview, getting off her second taxi on Jan Smuts Avenue and walking languorously down Hamilton Street in a neat new pair of black pants and a lemon-coloured shirt. She's early and has time to scrutinise the quaint gardens that stretch out in front of these wonderful houses like big, green welcome mats. She realises that you have to be someone to come home to a house in Craighall Park, to afford this kind of suburban bliss.

Walking further down the street, the humming traffic of Jan Smuts Avenue fades, leaving behind a fresh palette of sound; a whining bark of a small dog and the growing laughter of children. She imagines them jumping, playing and dancing in the still light of the early afternoon sun. She follows the trail of laughter, enchanted by its open, airy sound of trumpets, of freedom and inexhaustible joy. Soon she finds herself in front of the Never Never Land Nursery School and Day Care Centre and rings the bell. The name is painted across the top of a large building in bright purple, the rest of the wall is covered with a mural of fairies, little boys, ships and the sea. She doesn't wait long until the door flies open.

"Janine, right?"

Janine nods and gives a small, "Yes."

"Hi! It's so good to meet you. Come in, come in. I'm Melinda Walters."

"Pleasure to meet you," says Janine as she shakes the delicate hand.

"Shall I take you through?"

"Yes, please." She's eager to see what unfolds. Mrs Walters wears a pair of beige pants, a delicate peach blouse, teamed with a light beige cardigan. A string of pearls peeks through the ends of her blond hair as it feathers around her neck, and the faint smell of jasmine lingers around her. Every detail seems to be part of a well-worked out ensemble. But Janine's roving eye stops at her feet. Mrs Walters is wearing a pair of Crocs.

"Oh, I'm on my feet all day with the kids," she says as she catches Janine frowning at her shoes. Her face crinkles with embarrassment.

"My husband hates them too. But if you decide to work here, you will see how these shoes will save your life."

Janine only half-listens as she walks along the left wall which is lined with pigeon-holes painted in primary red. Each pigeon-hole has a small bright label attached to it: Lucy, Amanda, Jeanie, Margaret, Wendy, and then down the other side, Richard, Dean, Michael, Peter… Her eyes scan across these little lives as if they are small stories that she is about to read.

"You're nervous," says Mrs Walters, seeing her tense expression.

Janine is unsure how to respond.

"Don't worry, they are just children. I was going to say that they don't bite, but sometimes they do! We get some real terrors in here." She gently pats Janine on the bicep to reassure her. A light breeze blows and a wind chime clangs above their heads as they make their way through the back gate.

"And this is the heart of Never Never Land!" says Mrs Walters, presenting the entire backyard to Janine with an elegant sweep of her hand.

A black lady in a crisp maid's uniform moves about as she picks up the stray toys that are scattered all over the garden.

"That's Jackie, she works with the kids as well."

Janine watches meek Jackie flutter about in her neat apron and doek. "Would I have to wear … a uniform?" she asks, trying to keep the panic out of her voice.

"No, no, Jackie does all the cleaning up. I'm not hiring for that position."

Mrs Walter prompts her towards a bright purple building at the far end of the yard, and the smell of baby powder and waxy crayons greets her at the door.

They continue into a broad passage where the noise trebles and clarifies. They stop outside a room and look in through the open door.

"This is the two-to-four-year-old group. This is where I would like to slot you in, if you're interested," says Mrs Walters. "Elaine just can't cope on her own anymore. We've had such an increase in numbers in this batch."

Janine observes their rapid-fire attention spans that bounce off everything in the room.

"So, Elaine will basically run the show but you would need to help her maintain order and run the activities that have been decided on – the teacher's assistant."

"I think I can manage that," says Janine doubtfully and Mrs Walters laughs jollily.

"You know, being a mother myself, I have a sense about these things, about who you can trust around your children," she says as she bathes her with a generous smile.

Janine does not walk, but floats away. She sees a piece of a childhood she never had and laughs at the irony of having to grow up so that she could arrive at the gates of a place like Never Never Land. More powerful than nostalgia is the feeling of rebirth.

March 1997

Neha sits in the third row from the front, which is also the third row from the back. She imagines that she is most inconspicuous in the middle pew. She has felt that it is best to keep her intentions vague, secretly knowing that some semblance of a prayer has been building in her heart. She wonders if it will form itself, if these words will find courage here, in the place where Devon has always found his, to speak the otherwise impossible phrases of faith. She has come this morning to support him, to see him through his very first sermon. But the candles, the gentle Sunday morning sunlight that streams in through the doors, the lingering smell of incense, and the figure of Christ at centre stage with painfully outstretched arms, pinned in an expression of exaggerated generosity, creates an ambience begging for her murmurs.

Her plea is not a rational one, but lately she has found herself begging the gods whenever she holds Frik in her arms. She has no one to turn to but them, no one to ask to alter his intention of leaving the country when his degree is done. She cannot bring herself to ask him, despising what she sees as feminine clinginess, to stay. So she lets her heart pour out her irrational prayer to this irrational god, "Please God, please God." The words collect around the creases of her mouth as she softly sounds them out. She tugs uncomfortably at the dress that she has worn especially for the occasion.

"And now," says Father Patrick proudly, "I am handing over the pulpit to Devon who will be giving the sermon today."

Neha's heart jumps as she watches him in his sombre beige cassock. She sees him transform into something stronger, almost growing into his oversized robe. For the first time, she's able to recognise that this passion of his is something more than just a hobby or a quirk, more than compensation or even a tribute to his dead mother. It is him, her friend Devon, with his feet rooted in his compassion and his fingertips touching the sun.

Janine watches little Thabo who, like her, is a new member of Never Never Land. Thabo's parents are both doctors, but they have only just been able to move out of the townships and into the suburbs of Johannesburg. They are new to upper middle-class affluence and what it can afford them and their little Thabo. Janine listens to the singing chorus rise in the air. These little renditions always provide a thrill as she watches the children stand together like a choir of cherubs, their little mouths rounding out the letters in an exaggerated fashion. But Thabo struggles to keep up, his face melts and his eyes dart around in shame at his inadequacy. She thinks back on her own childhood – she too knew none of these things at four. These precocious children set the standard for all performances; they are the ones who will go on to become bankers, lawyers, doctors and actors. They cannot fail, nor are they expected to. She watches them, so blissfully unaware of how privileged they are, with some dismay. They have never had to catch two taxis to get to Never Never Land like she must. They were simply born into this dream and have never had to leave the fantasy behind.

Shejal fiddles with the commands of his computer programming assignment between bouts of virtual tennis. He chuckles to himself as he plays around with his design, a programme he has named G(o)od Dog; ironic of course, because the commands are set for it to disobey. More than that, he enjoys the double irony – a programme can never disobey. Designed correctly, a computer programme can rise to pristine and godly perfection. He has done really well on this assignment, which has now whetted his appetite to pursue an honours degree. But as the dream builds, he switches back to tennis to disengage: how can he explain *this* to his family? That he wants to continue studying, to postpone his eventual take-over of the House of Carpets to play with G(o)od Dog?

There is a rap on the door and it swings open.

"You and your computer," says his grandmother, making a tut-tut sound in the back of her throat, "never talking to real people, my boy."

He pauses to think through her accusation. He has not considered himself a recluse before, but she is right. He can't remember the last time he had a real conversation with anyone at home. And now as she stands in his room, expectantly, he realises that he has nothing to say to her. He lowers his gaze from her milky eyes, feeling embarrassed by the loss of language.

As his grandmother begins to feel obsolete in his space, she wanders off.

His heart aches, wishing people could have the easy fluidity of the computer whose readiness to receive new data and code, to experiment with languages and grammars that are almost always unfamiliar, is exemplary. The computer has no ideals, no culture and tradition – even the source code can be rewritten and replaced with a multitude of context-free grammars for purposes of adaptation and evolution. He hangs his arms around the monitor in an act of love and solidarity. The computer stands alone and unburdened, just like him.

January 1998

Kumari swiftly took the opportunity to work in an investment bank in Sandton after completing her BComm degree. There was no option of hanging around for postgraduate study like Neha – that was not part of *her* plan!

She wipes the sleep from her face and straightens her skirt as she walks into her crammed open-plan office. Her heart beats as she looks at her desk calendar; there is a day marked out in bold red marker. On the space allocated for 14 February she has drawn whimsical patterns, sketching little hearts around a G and a K. Govind has insisted that she takes that day off from work. That will be the day, she is sure of it, on which he will ask her to marry him. Her imagination conjures up a hundred scenarios; a hot-air balloon ride, a picnic in a park, a trip to Hartebeespoort, a big party with all of their friends and families, a quiet lunch in a romantic restaurant, or will he bungee jump off a bridge as a declaration of love for her, screaming The Question as he plummets towards the earth? *No, Govind will never do that*, she thinks, as she edits out the possibility.

Too giddy to work, she sighs with satisfaction. Her plan is playing out masterfully: a degree, a job and now, finally, a husband.

✳

Shejal tries to escape the smell of agarbiti that spreads around the house like a liquid snake. He sits on his bed, tugging at the white kurta that his mother has made him wear. He pulls at the white flaps of material that get caught under his thighs to give him freedom of movement again. He imagines the source of the ominous agarbiti, seeing the bunch of sticks standing in a brass vase in the living room, next to the garlanded photo of his grandmother. They pump out angry puffs of perfume and smoke, ceremoniously veiling her memory and her face. Shejal wonders how long it will be before the smell fades from their curtains and walls, how long until their food stops tasting like ash and their sight stops being hampered by the fog. But he retreats from that far moment in fear, too scared that he might actually miss his dead grandmother and feel a part of him that is empty. The shock forms a knot in the middle of his chest; he has not wept a tear. The muffled voices of relatives grow outside the door. Soon they will come. They will come to pull him out and hold him and want him to cry with them.

"You're darker than Alice!"

"Who's Alice?" asks Janine.

"Alice, my maid, Alice," says Amy, her face indicating that this fact is the most obvious thing in the world.

Janine frowns. They are called, in some capacity, to be second mothers to these children, not second maids.

"But you're not even black. You're Indian," she notes, tugging Janine's straight hair.

Blackie! Blackie! Blackie! It is the thing that makes everything exceptional. Janine – the darkest of Indians. A girl covered from head to toe in hot tar. Her skin is something that she has grown to think of as a rare kind of force-field, but the small, perplexed face makes her laugh, "Yes, but we come in all shades of brown. Now, why don't you go and play with the other kids?"

"No, I love you, I love *you*."

Janine tries to unwrap her arm from around her neck, but her tiny fingers turn into desperate claws. "Okay fine, but you promise me … that from tomorrow onwards, you will start playing games during games time, okay?"

"Yes-yes," says Amy. Janine heaves her up onto her hip so that she can walk to the jungle gym to watch over the rest of the children at the same time.

"You know, you know … my daddy flies jet planes," boasts Amy in an attempt to keep Janine's attention.

"Oh wow, that's so cool. And what does your mommy do?"

"I dunno. She has a boyfriend, so she doesn't stay with us anymore … I don't know what she does."

Janine pulls her closer, breathing in the smell of Johnson & Johnson baby shampoo that she has come to know distinctly since working here. She pulls a funny face at Amy, recovering the smile that has faded from her face.

E-mail! It makes her heart sing, the only portal that still connects her to Frik. A few letters passed between them before the commitment to letter writing became burdensome and the distance too painful. Now that they both have email addresses, their communication has been resuscitated. This is not to say that he e-mails her every day; he would never risk looking like a romantic sod. But she checks diligently – every day – for just a few words to shed light on his new life. Today he has e-mailed her not once but twice, each within an hour of the other – is it safe to assume that she has been on his mind for that entire time span?

"This place is just full of cold and darkness," he writes. "I spent a weekend in Amsterdam and couldn't help but miss you. Exploring life means little without having someone you care about to share it with you. You were nothing but goodness, goodness and sunshine to me.'

Her heartbeat elevates in tandem with the hum of the hard disk drive. These are the words she has been waiting for – an earnest reply to her longing. What took them so long? Why did they come so late? She remains caught between relief and disappointment.

Nevertheless, these warm rag words wipe away the ice that she has built around her heart, and now that she no longer wishes him dead, the minute details of his life take on an empathetic glow. It hurts her that he is struggling to settle in, to find a flat that suits his budget, even the saga about the neighbour's cat that keeps crapping on his front doormat makes her tense. She mouse-clicks closer to him, the Web pulling them together through these embedded tales that he plants in its huge field just for her. She wishes she could hold him, her alienated Frik, so lost in a world that he thought would be more like his own. He has no one to speak to other than her – she can now read that into the little narratives about how those people mock his dull pronunciation of Dutch and scoff as he explains the phenomenon of Afrikaans to them, laughing and dismissing it as an ancient form of Dutch, the kind their grandmothers spoke. She has always thought that she admired Frik for his decisiveness, but now she pities him instead. She knows that he will never return to South Africa – to her – not because he doesn't want to, but simply because of a misplaced sense of commitment to his ideals.

"Naheen, I'm not giving that price, that price is too low, too low," says Anup as he shakes his head. His greasy hair falls untidily across his face like a dark blind.

Devon sighs stubbornly, unwilling to repeat his offer to this cunning Indian who preyed on his earlier ignorance and has now come back for seconds. Anup is from India, one of the distributive goons in someone else's shady import business through which brass makes its way from India into South Africa, from there to here. Devon resents having Anup in his shop. He can smell the hot coconut oil grow rancid in the air as Anup sweats in the leather jacket that he always wears despite the season. He wishes he could source his brass as indifferently as he does his glass, through catalogues and cold dealers, but since all the brass comes from India this is the modus operandi – the middle man cannot be done away with, he refuses to be cut out from the cut. Devon suspects that it is people like Anup who prevent a more efficient system from being put into place.

"Please go," he says. "If you not willing to meet my price, then just leave."

"Bhaiya," says Anup softly, as if he does not understand.

The hairs on Devon's neck stand up. He hates it when they call him brother.

"Bhaiya, please," says Anup again.

"Please leave," says Devon, trying to curb his annoyance, insulted by the assumed relation. He scoffs as he thinks of the lives of these men who are all probably illegal aliens, who sleep twelve to a room in a cheap flat in Mayfair or Fordsburg, who always smell like coconut oil and biryani, who wear too-tight stone-washed jeans with fake brand labels attached to them and who call him bhaiya. But he is not their bhaiya, because his life is nothing like theirs. How ignorant of them to evoke kinship based on race alone.

"Bhaiya, please listen, nah. I got family in Srinagar and must send money home, to send my children to school, *English* school," says Anup.

"You want your money, then don't rip me off. The last time you sold me those same pots for three thousand rands and then you sell them to my uncle for two thousand!"

"Okay-okay, sir." His neck wriggles on a loose hinge like a bobble-head. "Okay, okay, sir, two thousand, sir. I will have no money left to send back to family in India. But okay … must keep good customer. Your father was very good customer and kind man, your father was," he says, keeping his eyes pinned to the ground.

Devon feels guilty for shouting him into such debasement. He paces uncomfortably, picking up the pots to determine their true value. He examines the fine craftsmanship and imagines the hot noises of small hammers and picks as they tap against the raw metal to bring these pieces to life. He imagines the trip they took across the sea, the bribes at customs that had to be paid – it seems almost miraculous that they ended up here, in his shop. He knows nothing of Anup's hardships; leaving an overpopulated country that is too poor to feed him and his family, working an exploitative job to support them. He wonders if all that unpleasantness would have had the same effect on himself, turned him into a cunning trader too.

"Ja, okay … I'll give you three thousand," says Devon, unable to take the crestfallen expression on the man's face. He quickly counts out the money from the till and notes it in his books. "There you go."

"Arre! Thanks, bhaiya," says Anup as he picks up his bag and leaves the box behind.

He waves from outside the shop and Devon sees a sneaky smile dance across his face. He kicks the box and the brass pots rattle. He knows that he has been taken for a fool again – for there is no mistaking that smirk of victory on Anup's face. He curses himself for his stupidity; emotional blackmail is not off limits to these vultures who after all these years still eat off the memory of his dead father.

February 1998

Devon undoes his robe in the office and walks into the church court-yard. He sees Aunty Benita talking to Father Patrick and passing him a worried look over the priest's shoulder. She has been giving him that same anxious look all through the service, but Devon dismisses it, think-ing that something must be going wrong with her wayward children again. He walks over to her, leaning in to receive his regulatory pruney kiss, but she clouts his face away from hers.

"Don't you kiss me," she yells in her frail voice and little glass pieces of her cough sweet drizzle all over the floor. "God sees everything, even when you doing the devil's work."

"Thanks, Aunty," says Father Patrick sternly. "I will now speak to Devon alone, thanks. Devon," he says grimly, nudging him into his office.

As soon as he shuts the door, he says, "I can't have you as a lay minis-ter anymore. Aunty Benita says she saw you, with a man, and the word *will* spread. I can't let this go too far, I don't want to have to take drastic action against you."

Devon looks away from the man that he has respected for so long, respected more than himself.

"I'm sorry, you know the rules," the priest adds.

"Yes, yes … don't ask, don't tell, right?"

"Someone asked," says Father Patrick with a shrug. "This is so diffi-cult … I have to be seen to enforce the policy … This is Aunty Benita's church too."

"Guh," Devon spits, annoyed that his spiritual and religious aptitude has been placed in filial relation to a bigoted geriatric.

"We can't just do as we please." Father Patrick kneels to meet Devon's downcast eye. "It's okay, it's not the end of the world. Just lie low and give it some time. We will take it from there." He rubs his palm across the side of Devon's face to calm him down.

✳

"Just gimme the rolling pin, Devon will be home from church now-now," says Janine as Kumari rolls out another roti into broken pieces of dough.

"No, lemme just try again," she replies, determined to learn how to cook now that she is officially engaged.

"You're pressing it too hard," Neha shrieks with pleasure, as though watching a cooking show that is falling apart. She turns to Shejal, expecting him to laugh with her, but is surprised to find him with his nose buried in a book. "What are you reading? You've been staring at it all morning."

"It's a diary." He drops it on the counter and she scurries forward like a dog.

"A diary! Ooooowwee," she howls, curiosity dripping from her vo-racious eyes. She opens the rough leather-bound book and turns the yellowing pages, drunk on the possibility of all the intimate details that will unfold before her eyes. She eventually settles on a page, but then complains, "Oh piss off, Shej, it's in some funky Indian script."

"I know. Dom, neh? It's one of my grandfather's diaries. My granny told my mother to give them to me after her passing. And can you believe there are eleven of these dik books? I got kak excited for nothing when I saw that two of them are in English. I started reading them, but I've just dumped them back in the box cos I think they're fake. I mean, why write two diaries in English? I know for a fact that he and my granny spoke Gujarati, so it doesn't make sense … and the English is so fancy, they're probably not even his diaries."

"But the rest are in, what, Gujarati, right? So maybe those are his real diaries then. I'm sure we can find someone to read them."

"You tell me who."

"How about the temple priests? They must know the language. If we find the right one. It's like Indiana Jones! We can all go back into the temple for the lost code," she adds, sharing the fantasy as it builds inside her mind.

"Just give it back here." He's irritated at how exciting she finds this bogus discovery. As far as he knows, his grandfather's life was anything but adventurous. It was just carpets, carpets and more carpets. There is a large part of him that feels grateful for this code that he cannot crack.

"Sjoe, brah, what took you so long?" asks Neha as Devon slinks into the house.

"I have to leave, I have to leave Lenz," he mutters to the sky, talking to some celestial being.

"Eish, as soon as I start my job, I'm outta here," says Shejal.

"I'm dead serious, brah, I *have* to leave. I can't stay here anymore." He shudders at the thought of that gossip making its way around the entire congregation. Father Patrick told him to be strategic and the only strategy he can now see is to flee! "One of the aunties at church must have seen me with David yesterday and she told the priest. Joh, dude! The whole congregation knows by now, I'm sure!"

"Hey, I thought you guys were breaking up," says Janine with a smirk.

"I was getting there."

"Mmm, sure."

Shejal passes the open bottle of wine to him. He gratefully accepts, grabbing it by the neck like a chicken for slaughter.

"You know," says Shejal, "if you wanna leave Lenz, then we'll join you. My family situation is so tense now that I've accepted a job offer from those software developers … I'm happy to leave it all behind."

"Ja, it makes good sense. Most of us have jobs now, so it's possible," says Janine.

"And hopefully Neha will also get a job someday," adds Kumari.

"Shut up, who asked *you*?" sneers Neha. "And for your information, I got a scholarship for my master's, I can pay my way, thank *you* very much."

"We could move somewhere closer to the city," says Janine, having already dreamed of such an opportunity.

"Where should we move?" asks Shejal, feeling hope drawing him in.

"Sandton!" suggests Kumari.

"Too expensive," says Janine.

"What about Mayfair?" asks Devon.

"Then we might as well stay in Lenz," says Shejal, "same shit, different smell."

"Who cares, anywhere but here!" Janine kisses him as her joy over-spills. "To the Five moving the fuck outta Lenz!"

WATER

February 1999

The champagne glasses clink, but Devon quickly abandons his on the table. He walks to the kitchen, his shoulder slamming against the doorframe that he has walked through and mastered all of his life. His eyes narrow as he assesses the items laid out on the kitchen counter: lime green plates, matching bowls, streak-free glasses, silver settings polished twice, olive napkins in copper rings. He stands, stares, not knowing which of this elaborate list to usher in first as a grand prelude to what will be their last supper.

Neha senses the stagnant sadness in the kitchen as she walks in. She pulls Devon's gaze away from the counter with a knowing smile. She picks up the plates and nods firmly at him to follow.

Like five pleats on a freshly starched dress, they sit down at the dining room table with stiff formality.

"My uncle has a van. I can ask him to lend it to you to move all of your furniture and stuff," says Kumari, relying on the never-ending to-do list to get them going. "Oh, come on you people! This is our last supper in this house, our last memory of a meal here, so just enjoy it."

"Kumari's right," says Neha.

"Yes, okay – just tell your uncle that we'll need the van after Wednesday. I'm only picking up the keys then," says Devon.

"I took the entire week off from work," says Shejal, "so I can help you."

"So, we're set then," says Neha, picking up her fork even though she feels her appetite wane. The silence consumes them again. They have made the plans and laid out the foundations, but no one knows what their lives will be, stepping away from the gruesome geography of murder, where the blood of an old man has pooled in the bedrock of their friendship, binding them in sticky awareness of their limited power in the world.

✳

Shejal sits on his orange carpet and slowly unearths the photo albums that are stored under his bed. He takes out these pieces of his past and slides them along the carpet to dust the front covers. The bindings creak with reluctance, wary of scrolling through these old memories. There is an entire album for almost each year of his life and another for every birthday that he has celebrated. The plethora of photos becomes arbitrary in their repetition of a single theme – *him*. It seems like a relentless case of paranoia, as if his parents wanted to keep a most recent picture in case he went missing. He convinces himself of this, struggling with the more simplistic and probable explanation – that they loved him *that* much, or wanted to remember his history *that* often and *that* fondly.

He flips through his birthday pictures. He smiles at the sight of himself and his young cousins clamming together like bodies of mischief in front of the camera. He finds it hard to believe that they could all get along and look so happy in each other's company. That they could dance and smile, play blind-man's buff and hide-and-seek together. There was only one division in life then: boys versus girls. Now there is the endless cutting, fractioning, defining and dividing as adult life blossoms in its complexities. When he last met his cousins, at his grandmother's funeral, even conversation proved to be difficult – a betrayal of the promise of these photographs. Photos, he sees, are good mirrors of the past, but unreliable reflections of the future.

He shuts the album and starts to stack them in a box. His mother walks in and stands close to the door. She says nothing, just watches him pack. Like a painter of guilt, she randomly comes in to check if the last layer is dry before proceeding with the next coat.

"Are you taking all of those albums?" she asks coldly.

"Yes."

"They're mine," she says, "not yours."

"What are you saying? They're all pictures of me."

"At least let me have them to remind myself that you weren't always miserable in this house," she says before she walks off.

Shejal sighs, feeling exhausted by this emotional weight. He sends the albums cascading across the floor as he throws himself onto his bed. Perhaps the little boy in the photos would choose to stay here instead; *he* is his parents' idealised version of their son. It was his mother who kept the camera ready for all the moments that she felt were important in his life, but this one, the moment of his leaving, she would rather forget.

He stands up and stacks the albums together, resolving to leave them for her – they are hardly his, are hardly him. He gives back to the creator what she has created and runs free without the burden of their fictions. But what begins to grow inside him is not just anger, but panic. He touches the true discord of the situation. Who is going to take his photograph now?

✳

Janine uses a single suitcase to pack. There is so little of her life to gather up before she leaves, again. She imagines herself as a character in one of those cartoons – like one of the Lost Boys or Huckleberry Finn – carrying her belongings over her shoulder with just a hanky and a stick.

She pulls out her clothing from the cupboards and folds everything neatly into the suitcase, treasuring each piece that she has bought with her hard-earned money. Once she reaches the back of the cupboard, her fingers touch the only thing that she brought with her when she left her parents' house so many years ago. She digs out the velvet box and opens it. She smiles as she recalls the emptiness that she shared with that paring knife; she smiles at its dormancy, its sharp blade trapped underneath an elastic strap.

She snaps the box shut and tucks it in underneath her clothes. She is a woman without a history. Her past is a blank slate, making the uncertainty of the future nothing to fear. She closes her eyes and sees herself moving into their new home, smelling the fresh paint as it dries to a crisp white. She sees herself walking into those cold spaces all alone and whispering intimate greetings to each of the walls. She fastens the buckles on her suitcase and is ready to go.

"You know, your mother and I were thinking that this would make a good guestroom."

Neha hates these jokes. Her father has been making them all her life.

"I just came to make sure that you're free tomorrow," he says. "I'll come home early so we can make it to the dealer to pick up your car."

"Thanks, Dad," she says with a smile.

"You deserve it, Love. We're so proud of you, your mother and I, a full scholarship!" he exclaims, still surprised at his daughter's capabilities. "So you and your friends are all organised?' he asks warily. "It's not safe nowadays." His head drops, knowing that this is not the world he wanted his daughter to live in. This is not the world he tried to fight for.

"I know, I know, Dad," says Neha. "I've been taking care of myself for years now."

"You see, you have me to thank for that, huh?" he says, his face creasing like a crumpled scarf as he laughs.

She gets up to hug him and is startled by the smell of an old man. What is it doing on her father's skin? She pulls back and grazes her cheek on his stubble, wondering when he stopped fussing about being clean shaven. Neha clasps his hands in hers as they hold one another's eyes for a while, each looking for the old innocence and invincibility. His eyes have grown dimmer and his once strong jaw has become rounder, making his face lose all the elegant and sharp slopes of drive, wit and anger that it once had.

"How old *are* you, Dad?"

"Fifty-nine next month. Oh hell, I can retire soon." He drops her hand and lets his back curve slightly as he sighs. "So, my dear…what will you do with a master's in history one day?" he asks in a voice much more regal than his own.

"Oh I dunno … apply for a PhD?" She throws the suggestion in the air to carry her where it will, knowing that landing a job is not high on her list of priorities.

"What a luxury! I should let your mother know that we raised a spoilt brat," he guffaws.

*

"Do you need some dishes?" asks her mother. "What will you eat on?"

"Ma, everything is taken care of, so don't stress, okay," says Kumari.

She turns restlessly between her cupboards, her bed and the boxes, wishing she had a more concrete way of going about things to soothe her nerves. She feels peeved at her mother's presence in the room, perceiving her to be the source of her anxiety.

She yanks her shirt out of her mother's hands, still hearing the disapproving remark that went along with it – too tight and too colourful.

"Oh, my dear. I always thought that this kind of goodbye would only happen on your wedding day."

"I've already told you, I can't wait until the wedding in December, I can't handle the traffic to work every day. And Govind and I haven't found a house yet, and who knows how long that will take. … I've told you so many times …."

Like her mother, Govind has also expressed his preference for the more traditional option where she leaves her parents' home only as a married woman and she is starting to crack from the frustration of having to justify her choices over and over again.

Elina enters the room with a batch of laundry held between her twig-like arms.

"Sjoe, Elina, you looking so thin," says Kumari.

"Eish … I am not healthy anymore. And you leaving now that it's your turn to look after me?" she laughs. She looks down at the pile of clothing on the bed. There is nowhere to place the new load that she carries. "Eh, your mummy is not helping you pack, neh."

"Ja, rather let Elina help you," says her mother, getting up abruptly before leaving the room.

Kumari clears some space on the bed and Elina off-loads the batch with a heavy sigh.

"No man, just give me the laundry, you sit there instead," says Kumari.

Elina doesn't refuse the offer, though she immediately starts picking up clothes and folding them.

"No, just relax, okay. I can do it."

"Ja, you old now, neh?" Elina looks at her admirably, as if only just noticing the woman Kumari has become. She relents, easing her shrunken frame against the headboard, pushing aside more clothes to make room for her body.

Kumari continues to pack in silence, but when she grazes Elina's bony fingers she grips at the knuckles, overcome by the amount of life she has squeezed out of that very hand over the years. Elina stirs just long enough for their fingers to interlace before her grip loosens again as she slips back into sleep.

✻

After spending the entire day reducing most of the house to a bunch of boxes, Devon goes for a walk, finding the emptiness of the rooms strangely suffocating. The cool, fresh air makes him sigh with relief. Still, he turns back to catch a glimpse of the house under the quiet moon. Everything seems so peaceful and he muses at the many storms this house has faced. His fingers grip the inner lining of his pockets as he grows slightly anxious, wondering if his parents would agree with his decision to sell their dream in favour of his. A sharp, stringy chorus of crickets rises in the crisp air. Moving in a straight line, he connects the dots of the streetlamps, his pace increasing. He remembers walking these streets as a teenager, confused, alone and sad.

He hears a vicious bark on his right and misses a step in fright. He turns to the dog, seeing the same silly Alsatian that used to bark at him every day on the way to school and church, on the way to meet his friends. He laughs, seeing it froth at the mouth in anger, its nose poking through the gate that separates them.

"Ja, dog," shouts Devon into the darkness. He turns to face it directly, spreading his legs apart and puffing out his chest. "Come druk! Come get me!"

He has not realised it before, but he will miss this dog. There are so many people who hate him now for what he is. Yet it is only the dog that makes its scorn known. Everybody else's contempt lies silent, is laced in politely stilted conversations.

He steps closer to the gate, lets the barking reverberate against his body.

On this crisp morning, the Five travel as a jubilant convoy of cars; each flick of the indicator gaining new meaning as it points them towards their new home. They speed along the N12 to Alberton. This area is the healthy compromise they found for themselves – affordable, different, and close to the city.

"We're home!" sings Shejal. He props his new digital camera on the bonnet of his car and calls everyone to come for a photo. They gather in front of the gate while he checks the frame, sets the timer, before bolting to take his place amongst them and their victorious poses.

"Mark this day, people," says Neha as she opens the huge lock on the front gate, "13 February 1999." She rolls the gate on its tracks with dramatic flair.

They squeeze through the maze of boxes in the lounge as they try to reach the blank spaces that are still so pregnant with possibility.

Shejal does not miss a beat. He captures everything on his camera; a close-up of Neha's face against her new bedroom wall, a long shot of Kumari dancing in the passage, a picture of Janine inspecting the kitchen cupboards, and one of Devon trapped amongst the boxes. With his new digital camera he can take hundreds and thousands of pictures. He can make himself and his world all completely meaningful and insignificant at the same time.

"Okay, so how do we do this?' asks Neha as she throws the painting equipment on her bedroom floor.

"God. Don't you girls know anything?" asks Shejal. He bends down to crack open a tin of paint for her.

"If you wanna help, then help, or else I can figure it out on my own."

Neha can already see her walls in her mind – bright green and bright purple on opposite sides. She has always wanted loud colours in her room, but her mother found the idea too eccentric. She copies Shejal, opening the green tin and stirring it as he has done with the purple. She pours some into a tray and dips the roller just like him.

"Ooh," she shivers, hearing the wet rasp of the roller as she strokes it against the wall and watches the white disappear.

"You know," he says as they find their rhythm, "I was wondering if you could help me with my grandfather's diary. I heard of a Gujarati priest at one of the temples in Lenz, so we can go to see if he can help. I thought you'd be the right person to ask."

"Oh, you're asking me? *Me?* Oh, Shej, I'm so glad you finally realised how valuable I am. Of course I'm in, do you seriously think I'm gonna miss out on this mystery? Let's go tomorrow!"

"Yes, that sounds good! And thanks." He shyly jabs her on the shoulder with the roller, leaving behind a bright purple bruise.

"My God, we've come a long way, you and me," says Neha, responding in kind, leaving a green print on his T-shirt.

"We have, haven't we?" he flicks the roller at her. "Now that you know your place, which is to help me!"

"Ja, I guess with time, *anyone* can grow on you," she quips as paint cascades across the room.

They send showers of colour in each other's direction and slowly an old memory is evoked in Neha's mind. She remembers Holi spent with her brothers, the many occasions during which they doused each other in colour and love. She smiles stiffly, trying to hide the soppy fact that Shejal fills pieces of the void that her brothers have left behind.

❋

Unsure of what he will find in the diaries, Shejal has kept this business from the rest. He has sworn Neha to secrecy, threatening to exclude her from the quest if she mentions a word to anyone. He parks the car just outside the temple grounds and they stop their excited banter, following an intuitive call for silence.

They admire the grandeur of the architecture; tall pillars with ornate filigree-like carvings transplanted from the heart of India to this unassuming plot of Lenasian soil. As they near the temple itself, they become aware of a magnetic buzz that emanates from inside. There are people singing an early morning bhajan inside.

They spot the priest turning camphor around a deity in front of the worshippers.

"Let's just wait," whispers Neha.

"Oh God, we shouldn't have come," says Shejal. The agarbiti smoke clouds his eyes and makes him itch.

"Just shh and wait."

Shejal slips one of his grandfather's diaries out of his bag, comforted by its weight in his hands.

"Hello ...um, namaste," says Neha, standing at attention as the priest strolls out of the temple.

His white lungi drapes around the ball of his waist. He lifts up the bottom of his white T-shirt and scratches his navel, eyeing them suspiciously. Neha continues talking although she is uncertain about how much English he understands. Shejal did not tell her that this priest is from *India*-India. She slows down her speech to try to make her request clearer. It is not of the ordinary variety.

The priest clicks his tongue and returns none of their profuse and anxious smiles. It is not often that young people approach him unless they need to bless their new cars or get married. His hand rides over the ball of his stomach to the ball of his head. He stands in front of them and scratches the path in his oily hair.

Neha and Shejal wait, wondering if he has heard a single word they have said.

"Show me this diary," he says abruptly.

Shejal thrusts the leather-bound book into his hands. The priest opens it, flicks the pages with a licked finger. He gives a few nods and grunts and hands the book back to Shejal. "You not Gujarati speaking?"

"No."

"What language you speaking? Hindi?"

"No, English," says Shejal.

The priest grunts again. "You go, back room. Wife is there, she will read for you and make translation."

Shejal and Neha thank him and walk on. They quickly spot the little outbuilding that stands in the corner of the temple grounds, but it is dead quiet, closed.

"I told you we'd be too early," says Neha.

"No man," says Shejal in a whisper. "I'm sure she is up, these holy people like to get up early. I mean, look how easy it is for Devon to get up, well … when he used to go to church."

She huffs under the weight of half of the diary collection. "You really didn't need to bring them *all* today. I mean … I don't think she can read and translate *that* fast."

"Oh, just give them here if you going to nag!"

"Shh," says Neha, spotting the priest's wife.

She walks out her front door, barefoot, her sari pleats clasped tightly in her left hand. Neha admires the collection of silver that hangs around her ankles like frills on a fussy petticoat. In her right hand she holds an oval, steel container. They watch as she goes to the nearest patch of lawn and slowly pours its contents onto the ground.

"What is it?" asks Shejal.

"I dunno, looks like water to me."

"Is she praying or something?" He watches the meditative, almost distant way in which she works.

"I guess, I think so …"

They do not dare to interrupt, and only make their move once she has gone back inside. Neha knocks on the door of the little house and the dry marigolds that line the top frame of the door begin to shake. It then opens with a squeak and two small faces appear through a thin gap.

"Hello," says Neha, first trying to ascertain if this woman speaks English. The heavy gold nose-ring, the thick kohl around her eyes and the plain sari are suggestions that she does not.

"Hello," says the lady softly and then the little face at the bottom parrots her mother.

"We just spoke to, um, the priest inside and he said to come and ask you to help us read this book. It is in Gujarati and we don't know Gujarati," says Neha slowly, feeling self-conscious about her English; about its pace, vocabulary and pronunciation. They all become foreign elements on her tongue, up for reconsideration. How much of it does the woman understand?

"Oh," says the priest's wife, still keeping the door half-closed as though she is scared that her daughter might run out like a wild puppy. "My husband said it is okay? He said for me to help you?"

"Yes," says Neha, "just now." She points towards the temple.

They hear the slight rustle of bells as she undoes the chain latch on the door. "I am Meela and this," she says as she pats her daughter on her head, "is Rucha."

"I am Neha and this is Shejal."

"Come," Meela orders, wiping her hands on the stray end of her sari.

They struggle at the door as they try to take off their shoes and hold the diaries at the same time. Neha grunts and moans with her hasty effort, bewildered by the graceful manner in which Meela seems to float across the ground.

"Come, sit." She unstacks three plastic chairs for them at the table. Neha takes the lead, does all the talking.

Shejal is quiet, seeing the uncomfortable effect his presence has on Meela; she pulls at the sides of her cotton blouse that is slightly too big for her, she makes sure that her sari pleats fall over her feet, and she never looks at him. Thank God he had the good sense to bring Neha along with him. He watches her try to get their request across and he knows that he made the right choice.

"I bring some breakfast?" Meela asks. Neha and Shejal glance at each other, both quite hungry, but scared at the prospect of what she will place before them and what they will be obliged to eat.

"I bring some, you try."

Neha beams at Shejal as Meela disappears into the kitchen. "I can't believe this is happening," she says, her eyes sucking in the intricate details of the overstuffed house. They take in all the artefacts of antiquity, the brass pots and clay lamps that clash against the kitsch; a frame with a picture of an Indian God, his trident glowing in flickering LED lights, and a picture of an Indian actress, posing with her finger to her chin, like an eighties sweetheart.

Shejal begins to sneeze as a stick of agarbiti spews up fumes from inside a brass jar. And with the smell of cinnamon and elaachi thickening the air, filling the entire house with the promise of chai, he begins to feel claustrophobic. He'd like to leave.

But a steel tray is put down in front of them.

"Eat, eat," Meela says, smiling before she runs back into the kitchen. Her daughter stays behind this time. Her small hands dart forwards and steal a piece of papad. Neha and Shejal laugh as they hear her mousy crunching underneath the table.

"Be careful, it's hot," says Meela, arriving with two steel cups that she places in front of them.

Invited by the sweet aromas that dance out of the steel vessel, Neha takes a sip and scalds her tongue.

Meela returns again, this time with something that looks like yoghurt. Shejal dips his finger and licks it. "Shrikand!"

Meela laughs at his joy.

"I love shrikand. It's been ages since I had some." He picks up his spoon, all his agitation dissolved by the food of his youth.

Meela takes one of the diaries and opens it. Her thin fingers feather along the pages as she reads, treating it with the same delicacy as she does her sari. She begins to giggle as she reads an extract to herself. "Hai," she coos softly under her breath and begins to blush. She shuts the book and places her hands on her cheeks. "I will read the whole thing for you, but not now."

"Oh, of course not," says Neha. "We were hoping we could leave the diaries with you and then you could translate, you know, write it in English for us?"

"Ha! Okay-okay. No problem, I have a nice English-Gujarati dictionary." The glow of her blushing is still ringing in her cheeks. "But my writing in English is very bad. I can make notes in the week, but then you must come and write, also double-checking meaning and English same time."

"So we must come back every week to write together?" asks Neha to confirm.

Meela shakes her head in agreement.

After thanking her, they leave, and Neha says, "So, do you think your grandfather was a dirty ol' fart? You saw how she blushed when she read from the diary, right?"

"I hope so," he laughs. Perhaps his grandfather had more spunk than he has given him credit for. But then he pauses for a moment. "You know, I was thinking that you could come on your own from now on … You're the best one to correct the English anyways."

142

"What? Why?"

"Well, I just hate the way she looks at me, like I'm going to rape her with my eyes or something."

Neha laughs. "Don't be stupid," but then she remembers how Meela flinched when Shejal accidently grazed her hand when handing back the empty bowl. She'd clearly been uncomfortable around him.

"Ja, okay," she says, enjoying the thought of spending some time with Meela by herself without the discomfort of male company. "Yup, that's perfectly fine with me."

✳

Today he is determined – he will not just drive past like a spy. He will actually go in. He has driven towards the church in Alberton numerous times, at first it was a rational mission to note down the time of the services, but then it quickly turned into irrational cowardice. He has spent time in his car before, scanning the faces that frequent this church on a Sunday morning, wondering if this almost completely white crowd might be willing to incorporate him into their idea of family.

This morning he makes a point of coming early to slip in unnoticed and he keeps his eyes down as he flips through the hymnal. He feels brown; conspicuous and brown. Yet, as the service begins, Devon feels a tangible sense of magic in the present as it offers him the comfort of the past. He feels grateful for the regular rhythm of the Anglican order of service. The standing, sitting, the kneeling and the bowing – he understands every inflection and genuflection of this ritual.

"Welcome," says the priest at the door, giving him a firm handshake as he exits.

"Thanks," says Devon shyly.

"And you are?"

"Oh, Devon."

"Glad to have you here, I'm Robert." He gives Devon's hand one more squeeze before releasing it.

As the congregation comes out of the church, they knit into cliques. Devon stands in the courtyard and listens to people laugh with each other. He chides himself for that goofy introduction: "Oh, Devon". He replays his words in his mind, thinking how foolish he sounded. He has never had to say "I am Devon" in a church before. There was always his mother to go before him and legitimise the presence of her son. Here he is an absolute stranger without merit or failure. He laughs; here he is just Devon, only Devon, a nonchalant "Oh, Devon", and perhaps this is more than he will ever need.

Kumari smiles at him as he pulls his grumpy face and keeps his eye on the road. The house hunt has set them off on a string of arguments. Every area that Kumari likes turns out to be too expensive, so now they begin to explore Govind's more pragmatic suggestions. Today they are driving all the way to Midrand.

"God, it's not even Joburg," she whines, although she promised not to. "Look how long this drive is taking us. Every day we will have to make this drive to work and back. Every day!"

"Well, *queen*, if you want a nice house of your own with a nice piece of lawn to grow flowers in, then you have to compromise. We're not in the big bucks yet, ey doll."

He has just started his new job this year. He imagines that a few years of work experience will set him up for greater things.

She walks into the garden of the show house and strides across the expansive lawn. It is much bigger than the patch she grew up on. *Is that not enough?* she wonders. Her eyes pass over the roofs of houses as they stretch into the distance.

"You know, we could probably get a house like this in the south of Joburg somewhere," she says as she sees Govind hovering behind her, trying to read her thoughts.

"If you don't like the house then just say so," he snaps.

She stays in the garden feeling lost on the large piece of lawn, so far away from the south of Joburg in which she grew up, so far from people she knows.

December 1999

Janine closes her eyes, sticks her head out of the window and breathes in deeply. "Mmm, palm trees and pineapples," she murmurs, revelling in the pictures that pop up in her mind's eye.

They started their road trip in the early morning and now in the flush of light they are zeroing in on Durban. The thermometer in the car records an astonishing 38 degrees.

"Sjoe," says Shejal, feeling his skin turn to water, "it's only idiots who come to Durban during the summer."

The breezy air from the coastline brings humidity. Their pores cry for salvation as sweat begins to pour.

"Oooh, I can actually taste the salt," shrieks Janine, caught up in the cacophony of sensations. Unlike the rest of them, this is her very first trip to Durban. Her very first trip out of Johannesburg! She imagines all kinds of tropical buds that blossom into colourful flowers and fruits. In just the thick air alone, stirring around her like soup, everything feels tangible; sea, sun and a hint of ripe bananas.

"God, this is going to be something," says Shejal.

Kumari insisted that her friends stay at her grandmother's house, despite the fact that it would be filled to the brim with her entire family.

"At least we will get to be part of the inner workings of the wedding," says Janine.

"We going to be thrown into the middle of Indian wedding chaos, you mean," says Shejal.

They drive towards the Indian township of Chatsworth and all along its rolling hills, finding their way towards Kumari, their missing companion.

"No wonder so many Durbanites come to Joburg," says Devon disparagingly as they reach their destination.

They have come to a residential area in which the small, dishevelled homes are hidden behind thick sheets of lush green vegetation, banana trees and moss. He can easily trace his ancestry to this place, to the indentured slave labour system, and to Durban. He would only need to go back about two generations to do so, but it feels very far from home. Despite the fact that everyone is of Indian origin like them, brown like them, it is as though these people can smell – sense – that they are alien.

Kumari is all hails and hallelujahs as soon as she spots them jumping out of the car and grabs each of them in turn. "You have no idea how my family is driving me insane." It is enormously comforting to be surrounded by people who don't see her as just another ornate statue to be put into place amongst all the other gods and goddesses during the pre-wedding prayers.

In the house there are people darting about in all directions, carrying every kind of obscure-looking parcel, box and piece of furniture. She pulls the Five through, shouting out the names of relatives they will never remember. Finally, she leads them into the kitchen. "My granny!" she sings.

It is the legendary lady, a monument in Kumari's mind, the pivotal person around whom all her childhood memories and moral instructions revolve. Her face is hard and dark. Her wrinkles are fierce; the ridges look like the sinewy strings in a dried piece of biltong. She wears a pair of old-fashioned glasses and her remaining strands of hair are slick, oiled against her head and wrapped into a stingy bun.

"Prabashnee!" screams her granny at the highest possible pitch. "Kumari, go call that stupid cousin of yours and tell her to set the table. We have visitors now."

Kumari shuffles down the narrow passage, calling for her cousin.

"I made chicken curry, mutton curry, roast chicken, dhal, rice, beans curry, potatoes and some roti," Granny says in an accent so thick that they struggle to keep up with her extensive list. "I asked Kumari about all yurls one-one favourites."

Devon sighs with relief; when it comes to Indian people, food always seems to break the ice.

"Ey, have a dop man," says Kumari's uncle as he storms into the kitchen and thrusts a plastic cup at Devon. He has a thick black moustache and wears a pair of Ray-Ban Aviator sunglasses, even though they are inside the house. "Come man, celebration time! Ey, you girls can have one also."

Janine and Neha look at each other hesitantly. Is this some cultural test to which the right answer is a refusal?

"Come on, man, join us, have one shot," he says, pouring for them in plastic cups. "I know you drink. Ey, Joburg girls are fast," he winks.

The girls drink. It is bittersweet – alcohol dashed with insult.

"Psst," whispers Kumari as she spots Janine standing in the passage, "psst, Janine!"

"Oh," she says, peering back through the small gap that Kumari has left between the door and frame.

"Shh, I don't want anyone to know I'm here. Where's Neha? Get her and come inside." She slams the door shut, scared of being dragged out amongst the throng of guests again. After a few minutes Neha and Janine barge into the room, similarly relieved to be rescued from the chaos.

148

"I just can't bear to go back out there again," she moans. "I'm so freaken tired. And it's been people, people, people *all* the time. God, I've barely had time to breathe. You know, to just sit and think about my wedding and the wedding night and all that jazz."

She collapses on the bed and pats either side of her for her friends to take a seat. "You know, Janine, I've been meaning to ask you, about, you know – *the wedding night*," she says shyly.

"Are you asking me about sex!"

"Oh, get lost. Now's not the time for 'Kumari's such a prude'…blah, blah, blah…" she laughs. "I'm getting married tomorrow and someone needs to tell me what the hell to do."

Neha doubles over with laughter. The surprise of this conversation is too much for her to handle.

"So…" Janine pauses. She cannot look Kumari in the eye and do this – lie. How can she tell her friend who has waited all this time, who has turned sex into a pure and precious act in the soft feathery duvet of her mind, that sex will hurt and bleed and sting and feel awkward and sloppy, that the insides of her thighs will pain from being spread out so wide like the drumsticks of a butterfly chicken, that her back will hurt from taking his weight, that a man's penis is a hideous thing to look at in the beginning, alien to her body, that a man pulls his ugliest face when he comes, that sometimes a man will fuck you and you won't even feel like you're in the room, that an orgasm is like a trophy that you earn and sometimes you will need to fight a man for it, that it can be foul and disgusting as you drown in your fluids, that sometimes it's a comedy and other times it will reduce you to tears! That sex is a bit like death; it causes you pain, stress and even blood before it becomes beautiful. That it is aggressive and mad before it becomes soft. And that you will always go back for more! How can she tell Kumari that?

"Oh, just be yourself and take it as it comes," she says, staring up at the ceiling. "I mean, it's his first time as well, right? So, just let it flow. The first time's always awkward but it gets *much* better."

Well done, thinks Neha, grateful that the question was not asked of her.

Kumari stands outside, veiled from the sun by the pallu of her sari. Its gold sequins draw shadowy dots across her face as she waits for Govind to join her. She wears the sari chosen by her mother-in-law; a heavy red silk with thick gold borders and silver sequins that make twists and twirls all along the rest of the fabric. She slumps under the weight of the work, feeling much too decadent, even her make-up feels like an exaggerated face of demure happiness stuck onto her own. *At least it hides my nervousness,* she thinks. She stands with a coconut cradled in the palms of her hands.

Govind arrives and hesitantly glances at her. "Sorry, man! My brother lost my scarf," he says, casting his eyes away from the veil that turns her face into a sacred entity.

"You look … wow!" she whispers as he takes hold of her arm. She has never seen him look this handsome. The sight of him in his cream-gold suit and the traces of kohl around his eyes make her feel impossibly lucky.

"Let's go get married," he whispers, gently nudging her forward.

They walk into the hall. The sounds of an anonymous Indian band blare through the speakers, crackly at the edges from the shrill horns. Her feet shake nervously under her gaudy red drapery. *Thank God,* she thinks, *that no one can see me.* Her knees feel like jelly. The weight of the coconut in her palms is too much to bear. She and Govind take their seats on short stools around the fire as the priest introduces them. *My wedding, my wedding.* She turns to glance at her parents who sit close behind her. They do not take their eyes off her. Kumari feels her lips stick together. The creamy lipstick makes it impossible to use her face with her usual freedom; she feels robbed of the spontaneity of her own expressions. *Please don't let it be on my teeth,* she pleads, now in close proximity to the gods.

"Are you okay?" asks Govind, and Kumari lets one hand free from the fur of the coconut to give him a reassuring squeeze around the wrist. She is still here with him.

They bend over the fire. Sweat trickles down her armpits and she can feel her blouse go damp. But, as if mesmerised by the hot lick of the flames, the rest passes in a blur. It is only the sweat that she remembers afterwards, sweat collecting along her brow. It feels like the onset of a fever – a long one, a strong one, she thinks, feeling her soul evaporate from her body. Or is she being burnt just like the beautiful carnations that they cast into the ashy grave of the fire? Although she has had her granny explain the symbolism to her many times, it has become vague and fuzzy in her mind. Why is she committing these flowers to the flames? Why are they throwing betel nut, camphor and ghee in afterwards – to burn into nothing? As if they are preparing some elaborate recipe for which none of them know the outcome. And why can Govind not watch when they hide her behind a white sheet and tie the thali around her neck like a heavy bell? Why a toe-ring that feels uncomfortable, a red dot and kum-kum along her hair-parting as if it is a bleeding wound? Why must she follow Govind as they walk around the fire? She submits from exhaustion, sending her body on to continue with tradition.

Neha, Devon, Shejal and Janine have been given front row seats. Unlike everyone else, therefore, they cannot forget about the proceedings on stage and pass their time gossiping and chewing betel nut and jeera.

Neha twists in her chair, finding it impossible to cross her legs in the sari that Kumari's aunty has made her wear. Beside her, Janine feels quite pleased with her look. She sits as still as possible, careful not to sweat hideous half-moons into the tight sari blouse. She feels ethereal in the layers of soft purple chiffon.

"The last time we saw Kumari on stage was at her Bharatanatyam recital," whispers Devon, taken aback by her classical beauty.

The burning of camphor, agarbiti and the black fumes from the small wooden fire create a dramatic shroud of smoke around the stage. They watch their friend disappear as the ceremony proceeds, slipping further out of their view and into the grey haze with Govind. None of them know what to make of this indescribable sadness. Even now, he has not grown on them.

April 2000

The last few pages of the final volume of the collection will be ready and their time together will end. After a year of careful translation, Neha is disappointed at the thought of losing these Sunday mornings with Meela. As she walks through the temple grounds she sees the priest in the open courtyard. He is already at work, blessing someone's brand new car. Neha waves, but does not inspire a wave in return. Rucha runs up to greet her. Neha lifts her up and coos along with the little girl. Meela stands at the door, watching them from a distance.

Neha steps over the threshold with the awareness of a ritualised experience. She takes off her shoes, smells the agarbiti and the spicy chai on the stove. Although this is just a house, the ordinary takes on a surreal quality here; the air seems denser, the smells more pungent and the tastes all foreign. Everything seems to symbolise a shift for Neha, a crossing-over which takes her away from the world she inhabits.

"Here, your last pages, you read now, nah, and tell me if everything is okay," says Meela. She proudly pushes the sheets of paper across the table.

"Oh my God! I can't believe we're done, after all this time."

She starts to read and Rucha pulls up a chair behind her. She stands on it, unloosens Neha's floppy ponytail and begins to brush her hair with a fine comb. Neha laughs, feeling herself being strangled as the girl pulls mercilessly through the knots. She let Rucha comb her hair once before and there has been no turning back. She dreads the smell of the coconut oil that the girl loves to rub in her hair, but the sweetness of having her head stroked by these small hands makes her open to the otherwise unthinkable.

"Wow, your English, it's so much better than when we started," says Neha, pleased to see that the previous mistakes have all been absorbed and corrected.

"Ha, and now you also understand more quickly what I mean to say also," says Meela, remembering the earlier frustrations they had when trying to get meaning across the barriers of language. "But you also taught me well, now I can teach Baby also before she goes to school."

"So…I guess we're done then," says Neha.

"Gee, all done – finish," says Meela as she shakes her head definitively.

After a long pause, Neha gulps down the last of her chai and makes ready to leave. She is reluctant to let go of this world that has developed around her like the soft walls of a womb. She catches a glimpse of herself in the mirror and runs her hand over the oily plait that Rucha has made. She laughs at the rudimentary reproduction of her mother's hairstyle that sits on her head.

"Hey, where are you going?" asks Meela. "Work is all done, now we can watch movie. Nice Bollywood movie! With Sharukh Khan."

"Ah, ja! Cool," says Neha, not having a clue who that is. "Does it have subtitles? In English?"

"Yes, yes, come. Sunday morning is *my morning*, so we can watch movie," says Meela with a grin.

Neha smiles, knowing what the phrase "my morning" means in Meela's world. It means that her husband will be busy and will not interrupt her, that it belongs to her and her alone to do as she pleases. It means that Neha can stay as long as she likes, there is no meal to cook or chore to attend to. *My morning*: Meela always speaks it with such decadence, the greatest indication of pleasure that Neha has ever heard.

154

The three women sit on the brown old couch that faces the TV in the corner of the room. Meela has brought in all kinds of things to eat – sweetmeats and a syrupy red juice. Neha settles on the crunchy papad, finding it the closest approximation to popcorn. The movie is an unintentional comedy for her; she finds the acting tacky, the sets plastic, the coincidences too outrageous and the drama melodramatic. She spends her time watching Meela instead, who is so deeply engrossed in the plights of the character that she does not even bother to shout at Rucha when she drops pieces of crumpled papad all over the floor.

Meela begins to tear slightly during the wedding scene. "Hai…" she says and sighs. "And you, Neha, when are you getting married?"

"Ha! I guess I haven't found someone to love."

"Arre! Where you come with this love nonsense, so romantic – like one movie, nah." She laughs.

"Hey, you love your husband, don't you?"

"No, not love, arranged marriage," says Meela, still laughing.

"So, what, you don't love him?"

"No, no … five years before I met you, I have, I had," she corrects herself, "an arranged marriage. No love-dove, all this feelings," she says as she makes strange gestures with her hands. "I do my work and my husband is happy. There are no problems."

Neha is shocked by her lack of sentimentality. This is not the picture she has of Meela, the doting wife, in her head. "So…" she says blankly, trying to figure this out. Here she sits, being made to feel like a romantic fool by a woman who watches Bollywood movies! "So, you just get on with your lives?"

"Yes, and now also I have my good baby – *this* is love," she says, looking at Rucha with a heart full of admiration. She plants a kiss on her daughter's head.

"Why get married then?' asks Neha, feeling disillusioned and uncomfortable. Love, for her, is the only saving grace of the horrid institution.

"See. It's simple, simple contract. Do your duty and work, but your feeling is for *you*. It is *my* heart," she says, using that possessive pronoun again with the same decadence as when she says "*my* morning".

Neha feels stumped by this revelation. How quick she is to laugh at these marriages, these women who turn themselves into glorified bartered slaves. But it is all a farce. A farce in which they play the part and keep what is most precious – their hearts! The radicalism of this blows Neha's mind as she thinks of her mother and Kumari. Women in so-called evolved marriages, women who give themselves body, mind and soul, who sell their labour and their love, who keep nothing for themselves. And, as Meela continues to laugh at her, she thinks of herself, who suffers still because she gave her heart to a man who did not care to have it.

"You know, Devon, I'm really glad that you decided to study with me. I mean, when I thought about starting this part-time degree on my own, I couldn't help fearing that it would be lonely, you know?" says Peter as he packs up his books.

It was not long after joining the church that Devon fell into active service again. He soon took up lay ministry and it was an even shorter time before Father Robert suggested this part-time degree in theology.

"When Father Robert came to me and said that he wanted me to convince you to join my theological studies, I knew you were a godsend," he gushes, "and it's all working out so well so far. These study sessions really keep me motivated." He grabs another biscuit from the plate before walking to the front door.

"Ja, I know, I'm glad I started too. I never got the chance to study, so it's nice to have a challenge like this."

"And who knows, hey? You may be our next priest."

"Oh come on, being a lay minister is fine for me right now."

Devon smiles earnestly as Peter drives off, his new study-buddy.

"So does your boyfriend Peter *know*?" asks Neha entering the room after eavesdropping.

"You know, no one goes around class asking people if they gay or straight, Neha. It's not a pre-requisite to be there. Everyone is welcome, hell, even you can come."

"Oh, your humour, it's touching," she says. "But *really*, Devs?"

"No, I guess he doesn't and it's not like it matters. It's all in the past and I'm not in a relationship," he adds firmly.

"It's just funny though, I look at you and Peter, having your little gay study sessions."

"Oh, you so bored with life, woman! What do you mean our gay study sessions?"

"Well, the little pats of encouragement, the little smiles. The 'Oh, let me sharpen your pencil' and 'I'm so glad I found you, study-buddy.'"

"Are you for real?" asks Devon as he laughs, watching her sigh and perform like a distressed maiden. "But, ja, I guess you're right. The church takes kindly to male bonding. Nothing wrong with that, is there?" he adds with a naughty smile. "It's all very innocent though."

"So it's like being on a rugby team, with all its homosocial nuances? Getting into little scrums of prayer, play ball and win for Christ," says Neha as she starts animating the scene for him.

There is nothing left for him to do but laugh at the absurd contours of life and he cheers wholeheartedly when Neha makes a successful conversation kick across the lounge.

"Mum's made a very special birthday cake," says her father as he places a whiskey in front of her to toast to her health.

"Oh, yay!" says Neha enthusiastically.

He sips his drink and closes his eyes, taking in the early morning sun. Neha imagines that this is how he spends his free time now, unwinding in this chair until the day when he will be completely unwound from a life of corporate dedication. She remembers the house; the corner in which she used to hide from her brothers, the couch under which she threw her lunch box and forgot about it until it started to smell, the touch of the smooth wood as they rolled marbles on the table, and the angry clang of the chandelier every time they played ball in the house. *Is this what it means to get old?* She observes herself developing a romantic eye for every object that helped shape her childhood into what it was. And yet, there is now a discordant blend of all things new; the house has been decked out with every technological appliance. The two kinds of ice in her glass were produced by the state-of-the-art fridge that her parents recently purchased. Neha laughs at the sleek, silver DVD player; she is sure they cannot operate it. She does not understand why two retired people would choose to refurbish their house. Her brothers have firmly emigrated to the UK and she has left Lenz; there is no second generation that will come to take over this place.

"So, this PhD next year," he says, "what's it about?"

"I already told you, Dad," she moans, enraged at his memory loss. *Not you*, she thinks, *not one of the smartest and wittiest men I know!*

"Oh yes, that's right. Sorry, dear. What about, did you say?"

"I came upon these old diaries that belong to Shejal. Well, they're actually his grandfather's diaries and I helped to get them translated and they are just so fascinating. The idea of history, you know the writing of alternative histories and its processes," she rambles on, feeling a trickle of pleasure just talking about it.

"I just hate that you've become so horribly consumed with the past."

Neha sees the familiar frown of disapproval develop beneath his black-and-white beard.

"You know," she says, "I'm so sick of this. Get over it. I don't want to get into politics, so sue me!" Why can't he leave her with the agony of deciding for herself? It is hard enough to do that, just *that*. "And besides," she continues, "history *is* political. At least I'm not raising hell or toyi-toying on the street."

"Maybe it would be better if you did. Your generation is just lazy, like a bunch of fat drunkards enjoying the fruits of many seasons of hard labour." He almost spits the words.

Neha retreats in anger. His sarcastic wit has churned into a grumpy cynicism that leaves a foul taste in her mouth.

"I know what you historians do," he says, "you just sit there and pick on the old carcass of oppression like a bunch of intellectual vultures until there isn't anything left of it but doubt."

Neha takes a sip of her bitter drink. It stings her palette. It burns her throat. She gags.

"Soft, all gone soft," she hears him mutter again, as if to provoke her.

Devon and Peter stand together, having established each other as a firm source of company at the after-church tea table.

"Jesus," says Peter as he pulls off his stuffy blazer. Then, "God," trying to deal more directly with the source as he feels himself wilt in the sun.

"Let's go stand in the shade," says Devon.

"Devon, Devon," calls Father Robert, waving him down. "There is someone I would like you to counsel."

"Me?"

"Yes, he's a new member of the church, I'm sure you've seen him around. Well, I was thinking that maybe he would prefer to speak to someone younger, you know, more wit' it," he says, trying to use his hand like a hip-hop star.

"I don't like rap, if that's what you mean."

"Oh, no need to laugh at an old man," says Father Robert. "It's just that when he came to speak to me, I got the feeling that he wanted to say more, but was too intimidated or something of that variety. I think he will be more comfortable talking to you, and it will be good training for you. So is it okay? Can I arrange that?"

Devon's mouth opens and then closes again, without sound.

"I trust you," says Father Robert. "The point is just to listen."

"Ja, okay. Okay."

"Great," he says walking off in a hurry.

"My, my," says Peter, impressed.

A cool breeze blows through the old jacaranda tree, showering Devon with its limp purple blossoms.

"Shut up, you do this all the time with your youth group. This is my first time."

"Ag no, hardly the same thing, never did a one-on-one and never with a stranger."

Devon smiles at Peter's attempt at modesty, but it is clear that he is the better half of their duo – if Devon can even count himself as a whole half. Peter is a member of so many activities in the parish; he's a lay minister, youth leader, cell group leader and soup kitchen volunteer. He has even started learning the guitar so that he can join the music team. Devon cannot help feeling auxiliary next to Prolific Peter and he wonders why Father Robert has not more easily passed this assignment on to him.

"Ah, there they are!" shouts Father Robert in a theatrical strain, as if seeing them for the first time today. "My deacons in training. Devon, Peter, meet Owen. I was just telling him that hanging around us old people is detrimental to his wellbeing, so I thought it best to show him the young ones before he runs away from us altogether."

Devon shakes Owen's hand. He immediately understands why he is his assignment and not Peter's. Owen's eyes flit nervously as they make conversation and his handshake feels like grasping at cotton wool. His shoulders hunch forward and his head bows as if an invisible entity keeps whispering shameful secrets into his ear. More than that, Owen is also Indian. Devon wonders if this is Father Robert's summation of him: shy, uncertain and Indian. As Owen smiles and readies to walk away, Devon gives his number to this miserable mirror of himself.

✳

"You know, we told Neha she could invite anyone she wanted," says Janine, "but she just flat out refused and claims to have no friends. What kind of a person spends so much time at the same university and makes no friends?"

"Well, you know Neha. She's a loner," says Kumari.

"Strange, if you ask me. Anyway, I just spoke to Shejal and he is so excited about this mystery present for her. I mean, I've never seen him get excited like that about *anyone's* birthday except his own."

Kumari laughs. "Ain't that the truth! But what's this about? Shejal … and *Neha*?"

"No!" shouts Janine. "I mean … don't you just find it a little strange that they are so buddy-buddy with each other? And now he is all excited about picking out her gift? I mean, this is Shejal for God's sakes. Sometimes I have to wait months before he actually remembers to buy one for me."

"Jealous!" says Kumari. "You're jealous … of *Neha*? Come on, you're being silly now, Janine."

"I'm home!" sings the birthday girl as she pops her little frame into the house. She sees the two standing together, beside the table. The light apple green setting has been placed in her honour. It is her favourite colour.

"Oh, Kumari," she says, moving in for a hug, "thanks for coming over for lunch today! We really miss you around here, you know."

"We'll eat soon. We're just waiting for Shej and Devs. They went to get your gift."

"Oh my God, I can't wait!" She claps her hands with glee. "Aw, that Shej! He's really become a dear to me."

"How so … *exactly*?" asks Janine.

"Huh?"

"How … has he become a *dear* to you?"

"Well, the fact that I've been helping him out has made him more civil, I guess."

"Ja, what are you people up to exactly?"

"Ah, that's for Shejal to tell you, not me, not my business."

"Ja, but he doesn't tell me, so I'm asking *you*."

"Oh God, can we talk about something else?" asks Neha. "If he doesn't wanna tell you, that's your issue. Really, don't involve me in your relationship problems."

"Who said we having *problems*?' asks Janine, her sentences getting shorter and sharper.

"Please, Janine, don't insult me by involving me in a bitch fight for Shejal. Well, for any man for that matter … but *Shejal*?"

"Hey! He happens to be my boyfriend, okay. So don't talk about *him* like that. I hate it when you do that. Always dissing him and shit, like he is so beneath your high and mighty standards," says Janine rising up from her chair. "Fuck! No wonder you're alone!"

"Joh … Greyville gedagtes," says Neha. "You can take the girl out of Greyville but you can't take Greyville out of the girl."

"Oh please, just stop this shit!" says Kumari.

"You know, it's women like you who make me sick," says Neha. "I'm not your enemy, bitch, I'm your freaken friend!"

Yes, this is what bell hooks would have said if she were here, thinks Neha, feeling righteous, but hardly close to feeling like a winner.

✳

It takes just one look in those wary brown eyes for a new apex to rise in her heart. It is as if the party continues around and without her. She spends the entire evening with the small body tucked against her chest, glad for the flat breastplate between her two sorry excuses for boobs. She lets the warm puppy breath intoxicate her and its saliva baptise her into a new experience of life. How can she ever be alone now that she has her dog with her? Her empty space has already begun to take on the very size, shape, smell and colour of this beautiful Labrador puppy. She undoes the bow around his neck and he rewards her with a gentle lick on the nose.

"So, what will you call him?" asks Janine. She's irritated that a bunch of adults can spend an entire evening cooing over a puppy. Shejal hates dogs, it is beyond her how he could buy one for Neha and feel so pleased about it.

"He's *my* boy, right?" says Neha. "So I'm calling him Jairam Rajprakash."

Shejal roars with laughter. This is his grandfather's name. "Oh, it's too hilarious!" he hoots as he tries calling the dog to him.

November 2000

Her father rushes to fetch Kumari. It is the comfort of having another adult to shoulder the crisis that makes him drive all the way to Midrand in the early morning.

"It's Elina…" he said before he hung up the phone.

In the car he adds nothing more; she has been sick for months now.

Kumari walks into the little Wendy house. Only the afternoon sun, which droops with the weight of a ripe fruit, manages to squeeze into the small, single window. Now, during the dull morning, a candle burns. It sits on an old oil drum that Elina turned into a bedside table. Kumari's mother sits on a stool, holding a damp facecloth to the sick woman's forehead. Elina's eyes open – slowly and reluctantly – swollen and heavy with sleep.

"Why haven't you called the doctor?" asks Kumari.

"No, no, no doctor," says Elina with a feverish moan.

"*That's* why," says her mother. "She keeps insisting that she doesn't want to see one!"

"No, no … no," continues Elina, using a jolt of energy to turn her head from side to side.

"I've been checking that she takes her medication and I've seen to her meals and everything," says her mother, at her wits' end, wondering what more can be done. She takes one more look at Elina and another at Kumari and then flees, leaving her daughter to take up the vigil.

"Elina," Kumari says, stroking her face. Her fingers run across hard and rocky ridges; these are not the soft, pregnant slopes and valleys that they used to be.

Photographs of children still line the wall on the side of Elina's bed. Kumari glances at the one of her and Elina smiling in their naive glory.

"I don't understand you, why haven't you taken her to a doctor?' Kumari yells at her mother who sits helplessly at the kitchen counter, hunched over a cup of coffee.

"We wanted to, but she kept insisting! *You* saw her."

"She's delirious, who listens to someone who's delirious?"

"You know, we sent her home because she was ill. I mean, she has a family… Aren't we just employers? Aren't we supposed to let *them* take care of her? I mean, if *you* get sick, it's not your boss who's going to look after you, it's us! *She* came back, she came back *here* … sick as a dog and I don't know why!"

"So, what?" asks Kumari. "We just let her die?"

"And we *have*, we have taken her to the doctor, so many times," her mother adds fretfully.

Kumari grabs the edge of the blanket at Elina's head and her father carries at the feet. They puff and heave as they slide her rigid frame onto the back seat of the car, neither of them realising the true weight of bones until now. It feels barbaric, but this is the only way they can shoulder her weight alongside the weight of her protests. Kumari slides herself in on the back seat and props Elina's head on her lap. The sour breath of sickness reaches her, Elina's throat stretching along her thighs and her mouth jutting open. Kumari holds her firmly against her body as her father drives towards the Chris Hani Baragwanath Hospital in Soweto.

They wait for hours in a busy corridor of emergencies; broken arms, infected sores, emaciated people with chests heaving heavily, a little girl going in and out of consciousness beside a hysterical mother, a man holding a piece of cloth over a bullet wound. There is no hierarchy when it comes to people's pain. No one here can claim to *need* to cut in the queue like in the line at a girls' bathroom in a busy nightclub. Dying is a common fate, and in this cramped hospital building they have all come to accept its inevitability.

The doctor talks very little – in abrupt bursts – before he scribbles on a page.

"If you ask me, it looks like the final stages of full-blown AIDS – I mean, along with everything you've described to me … But without a blood test we can't say for sure," he says, pulling the curtain across as another patient takes the space next to them.

"Elina, we made you take a blood test, remember, remember last year, you took a blood test at the doctor and you told us you had no problems, that everything was okay?" Her mother pleads for an answer that does not come.

The doctor says, "Ma'am, it's the patient's decision to disclose their HIV status." Then, speaking as though Elina is not in the room, "See, I'm sorry, I can't admit her. We will do her blood work, but if she's HIV positive then I'm afraid we're going to have to release her. Because then, if this is just likely to be the symptoms of TB from a full-blown case, then there's nothing that can be done in terms of treatment but to alleviate the symptoms. I'm sorry. I suggest you contact the family and try to find a space in an AIDS home for her … Beds are too few here, ma'am. We try to save them for the people who have a chance."

Another room: the hospital unfolds like a large dormitory of death, room after room, bed after bed, chair after chair are all lined up. Elina sits in a chair with a piece of cotton wool on her arm, like all the other patients. Kumari stands lodged between her parents. They are pinned together by a skewer of fear. No one sees the insides of a hospital like this; the ugly intestine of the country in which no camera will roam. They are just figures and statistics; people that add up to a number with a percentage mark at the end.

A young man wearing a beanie riddled with holes walks up to them. He carries a younger boy on his hip although he is much too old to be carried. The young man goes over to Elina and whispers in her ear. She responds by putting a frail palm to his cheek.

"This my brother," he says, assuming they already know who *he* is.

It is only Kumari who can recognise him from the photographs in the Wendy house – he is one of Elina's sons.

"She said to me it is TB," he says as they all stand together looking down at her. "She said to me it is TB," he says again, in a whisper this time. "I work in Carletonville. I am a driver there. I take her home today because today I don't work."

They take this as their cue to leave. As they make their way out of the building, they take in thick wafts of the industrial cleaner that washes out everything except the feeling of sordidness that they carry. Out of the monstrous hospital, into the parking lot and through Soweto, they do not give in to the temptation of calling this an act of bravery or goodwill towards mankind. It was desperation that drove them there.

✳

As she lives through the moment she already knows that she will remember it for the rest of her life. She sees him striding up to her, his hands moving briskly at his sides, the sun shining around his frame like a glorious halo. She records it in her mind as one of *those* moments. Those moments when reality bursts open like a volcano and spits hot lava across one's front lawn. In the distance, she can already see the fine tailoring of his navy-blue uniform and the gleaming gold badges pinned across his chest.

"Captain," whispers Janine to herself as she sits, building a plastic pyramid with the children in the garden.

"Hi, hey, you must be Janine, right?" he asks, now towering over her, blocking out the sun.

Her brain shrieks and her heart stutters as he mentions her name. She is grateful to be on the ground already so that she does not have to feel her knees fold like spaghetti in a hot pot.

"Amy's told me so much about you," he says. "I recognised you from her descriptions."

He smiles and displays a soft cleft in the centre of his chin, like a fingerprint on the surface of setting jelly.

"Oh right, you're Amy's dad, the pilot."

"Ja," he laughs as he glances at his uniform. "You can call me Ben. This weekend is mine with Amy, so I called her mom and asked if it was okay if I fetched her from school a little earlier than usual."

Janine dusts off grains of sand stuck to her palms. "Well, then let me go and get her."

He leans in to whisper, "The thing is … I came, in part, to speak to *you*, Janine. Amy happens to like you a lot, you know. And, well, I work a lot and I only get alternate weekends with her for the moment and sometimes I can't make it because, well, I don't control the flight schedules. The thing is though…" He cranes his neck even further. He is now so close that Janine can pick up the woody aromas of his aftershave, the sweetness of a piece of damp bark. "I hate cancelling a weekend with Amy because her mother is just waiting to push a charge of negligence on me. So I came here specifically to talk to you because I know that you can help me with my situation."

"Really? How?"

"You could babysit from time to time. Like on those weekends when

I'm supposed to take Amy and I have to work. I thought you could just come over to my place and take care of her? I try to fight for my time, so it's usually just a night that I miss, at the most. I would never need you there for an entire weekend."

Janine waits for a moment, thinking. Amy is a handful.

"I will pay you generously, of course, because, well, employing you will be absolutely convenient – you're trained, Amy adores you and it's perfect because if I can't make the Friday then you can take her straight home with you, to my place, or if it's the Monday then you bring her in to work with you."

"It's just, I'm not sure the school will be okay with it," she says. "It might look like favouritism, or something."

"Ja, I know – I thought of that. What do you say we keep it between us?"

"Ja, okay," she says softly. "I'll do it."

"Hi. Hello. Come in," he says, opening the front door for Owen.

He's wearing a blue T-shirt that blends perfectly with his faded pair of jeans. Devon can say little for his spirit, but his sense of style is impeccable. The colour makes a handsome contrast with his brown skin and the warm timidity of his eyes.

"Thanks for inviting me over. I'm new in Joburg so I don't know a lot of people," he says, handing over a tin. "They're biscuits, I baked them myself. I have a lot of time on my hands," he adds with a nervous laugh.

"So, you're from Durban then?" asks Devon, picking up a trace of the accent in Owen's speech.

"Yes, I moved here to look for a job. I studied fashion design, so I thought I would find better opportunities here."

"Did you manage to find something?"

"Well, yes. I'm the assistant to one of the buyers at Truworths. You have to start somewhere, right?"

"Well, ja. We all do. So how you finding it here?"

"Well, fine. Just … well, lost …"

This is it, he thinks, *this is it! The sheep is lost – Oh God, what do I say now?* "Lost … how?" he squeaks.

Owen gives him an intense stare and starts to speak again. "You know, when I was still in Durban my mother joined this church and then, over time, I started going with her and it felt really good to be part of the community, even though I didn't think it was my scene."

Devon relaxes a little, there is not much talking for him to do now that Owen seems to be treating their meeting like a confession.

"And then, they sent me to all these camps and retreats and prayer groups because I was gay, you know."

Devon chokes on his coffee. "You were gay?"

"Yes. But then I got saved and cured and I was okay."

He takes a loud breath in. His heart races as his mind begins to wrap itself around this coincidence, confronting him with his own dread.

"But now that I'm in Joburg I feel myself slipping, like God is abandoning me. That's why I joined the church again. I don't want to feel lost or disgusting. I just want a normal life," says Owen as he looks up at Devon for a response.

"You know, you just have to relax. I think you're being extremely hard on yourself." He is speaking as much to Owen as to himself, though he can't think of any words of real comfort. "Would you like me to pray with you?"

He places a hand on Owen's shoulder, wondering what it is, exactly, that he is supposed to be asking God for – a cure? He looks at Owen, his head pinned to his chest as he awaits healing.

*

Neha slaps Shejal on the back. "Come, come," she chirps.

Shejal follows her into her bedroom.

"Ta-da-dum," she announces as she reveals the translated volumes of his grandfather's diaries. "I had them edited, printed and bound! So you won't have any more excuses for not reading them."

"Oh God! *Wow…* thanks," he says, seeing how much care she has taken with the covers alone.

He slowly pages through each of them, feeling the careful and diligent work of Neha and Meela and the hours they must have spent with his grandfather's words. The humble turns of history become tangible and seduce him with their quiet inspiration. As the opportunity slowly materialised to know his grandfather, he retracted from the diaries with a series of excuses. That way his grandfather could remain a mystery. He could be a freedom fighter, a poet, a politician, a rebel, a lover, a warrior or even a forgotten hero. Yet the extraordinary, he begins to see, lies in the acceptance of the mundane. Undertaking the journey to see his grandfather as a man bound to the failures and successes of his circumstances means that he must then also accept his own mortality. He warms to the idea that this may, in fact, be a more honest form of bravery.

"Now stop Hamleting about the thing already. Avenge! Avenge the ghost of your grandfather! You must read, Shejal," Neha announces in a ghostly boom.

Shejal thanks her again and heaves the entire collection to his own bedroom. He finds Janine sitting on the bed. He pauses for a moment, then puts the books down beside her.

"You know what these are?" he asks, deciding to finally let her in. "They're my grandfather's diaries."

Janine folds her arms. "So what?"

"No, in English. Neha helped me to get them translated."

Janine blinks and then sighs. She is not surprised that he has kept this silly little secret from her – she is not a part of his family. That same family that has left behind such a huge hole in his life, though admitting this to her would make him feel too vulnerable. She runs her hand over the books that Neha has had bound so beautifully and she giggles, thinking she should start being nicer to her again.

Shejal takes her hand. "I was hoping we could read them together, you know, a little at a time."

February 2001

Janine gets up early after a fitful night's rest in a strange bed. This is her first overnight stay in the Montgomery house to babysit Amy and she feels uncomfortable rummaging through the pantry like a raccoon. She quickly crunches down on a staunch bowl of cornflakes and milk for breakfast, then walks to Amy's room to check up on her. It is a pink palace; a room that puts no price on love for this child.

"Janine!" calls the little head, popping out from under a pink Barbie duvet.

Amy draws up and stretches her arms around Janine's neck. Janine obliges her. It is hard to draw the line when you are in the childcare business. A good morning kiss, a hug – these are all beyond the call of duty, inappropriate. But caught in this innocent grip, Janine gives her a soft hug in return before she rips the entire duvet away. The rush of cold air causes a large scream from the tiny body.

Later, she has managed to get Amy bathed and changed when the Captain enters the house. She watches him drop his cap on the table along with his car keys. He smiles at the sight of his daughter and Janine on the couch enjoying the Cartoon Network together.

"Can't get her away from that thing," he laughs, "but it's not exactly safe to let her ride her bicycle in the streets."

Janine nods, familiar with this excuse that parents give themselves for allowing their children to grow up and fat in front of a television.

"Mummy doesn't have DSTV," moans Amy.

"Well, Janine, there's nothing left for you to do, thanks again," he says, handing her a sizeable envelope. "I hope this arrangement continues to work out for the both of us."

His smile, coupled with the delicate, damp wood cologne, makes her weak-kneed. She turns to the TV in time to watch the roadrunner get smashed by another anvil.

✳

Kumari sits with her mother in the lounge. Three elderly black ladies with blankets tied around their bodies and doeks on their heads arrived at her mother's house this morning. They claimed to be Elina's relatives and came with The News. She is dead. They are now working in her room, cleaning out the few belongings that she acquired during the years spent in the little Wendy house in their backyard.

"Should we go and help them?" asks Kumari, not sure what to do.

"I already asked and they said it's okay. But should we give money? You know … for the funeral?"

"I don't know."

"I mean, we paid for her burial policy… but are we expected to pay – again?"

There is a knock on the back door and Kumari's mother jumps up to attend to the ladies. "Yes!" she says, as if they have startled her.

"We are done."

They hand over the key and remain standing at the door.

"Um, do you want to come inside?" asks her mother.

"You know, Masechaba works here all her life, and now there is children, three must still go to school," says one of the ladies.

Kumari's mother nods sympathetically, grateful to have a cue for something she understands. They are asking for money.

"Yes, I want to give you something, just as a contribution." She leaves to find her wallet.

The ladies stand silently at the door and Kumari goes to stand with them so that they do not feel abandoned at the doorstep that they refused to cross.

"Eh, how many children does eh … Masechaba have?" asks Kumari, feeling uncomfortable with the name she has never used.

"Six. Three are working and three are still in school, but now we don't know if they will have money for uniform, for books."

Kumari nods, wondering just how guilty she and her family are meant to feel. Undeniably, they were the ones who robbed her children of a mother, but they were also the ones who allowed her to pay for whatever little education and food they had. She goes back and forth in her mind until she trips on the memory of the old man who, like Elina, did not make it out of Lenz on time. There is no amount of rationalisation that can scrub her conscience clean and she wishes she could just ask about Elina. Nobody ever phoned after that day in the hospital to let them know how she was doing.

Kumari's mother returns and hands over a folded bundle of notes. The lady who accepts it curtsies slightly at the knees. The other two pick up the suitcases that stand at their heels. They leave without a word.

"Sheesh, Ma, that's a lot of money."

"I will feel less guilty this way."

They sit together, absent-mindedly sipping tea. Kumari thinks about what it would be like to drive through a dusty township and stand amongst the thick crowd of black people to say goodbye to Elina. She can see the hostile eyes piercing them; the murderers, the ones who worked her into a skeleton and sent her home to die. How ludicrous it would be to attend the funeral, she thinks, to go and commemorate the life and death of Masechaba whom they spent all of their time with, but never knew.

A new pattern has developed for Shejal and Janine. He no longer plays computer games or surfs the internet for hours on end until it is time for bed. Instead they curl up to read the diaries together. Janine has grown especially fond of his grandfather for this reason alone.

"Oh my God, what is this? I'm convinced he is the most boring man to have ever lived," says Shejal. He drops the book on the bed.

Janine laughs. The journal entries look more like ledgers; the work of someone taking the term 'personal accounts' quite literally. The pages do not reflect on his experiences, but rather serve as a log of his earnings, his desired earnings, money coming in and money going out. They are all tediously recorded in these books, accompanied by sporadic notes and lists of things to do and things to buy.

"Neha! Neha!" Shejal screams. "I'm gonna bliksem this chick, man."

"What?" she asks, poking her head into their bedroom.

"What the hell? Why did you make me so psyched about these stupid diaries?"

"Because Jairam rocks!"

"Look at this! Numbers and lists! Who cares?"

"Oh God, you're still reading volume four. What slowpokes." She shakes her head. "Just keep reading. Things are about to change for Jairam, trust me."

"That's what we've been doing," says Janine with exasperation.

It is a plea for help and Neha jumps up on the bed, deciding to aid them along. She reaches for the first volume of the set.

"See," she says, opening the book as if it is all self-evident. "I remember you telling me that your grandfather first worked in his father's shop, right? A general supplies store in Durban Central … that's what you said. So if you look at this, it's more like the accounts for the shop. I mean, look at the listings and the amounts. The quantities are much too large for just a family. They are more than just grocery lists – it is an inventory for the shop." She runs a finger over the figures. "Can you just imagine how stressful his life must have been? A young boy, trying to keep track of every bit of money that passed through his hands?

"And look at this," says Neha pointing out a pattern, "at different intervals you see a sum of money written in a block in the side margins. This, I think, is part of his personal savings. See how it grows slowly as he moves on?"

Shejal and Janine diligently flip pages to watch the blocked out sum of money grow.

"I mean, I think that is his personal money because if you look at the end of volume four … there," she says as she finds the page. "See … this money in the block makes the first purchase of carpets! This is the money your grandfather uses to buy his very first quota of carpets, his initial capital for what is now your great business to inherit, if you please."

Shejal runs his finger across the word that has haunted him his entire life: carpets. The thought of it still fills him with disdain. "What is this? Dockside Wallah?" he asks, looking at the inscription beside it.

"Well, I did some secondary reading and I think this is the person your grandfather got his carpets from. The carpets all came from India by ship at that time, so I guess Dockside Wallah is one of the guys who would get them off the ships and into the shops." Neha turns the page. "See, there you go … your family's first carpet sold for three pounds and forty shillings, which was a killing in those days. And then as you go on, the frequency with which he buys and sells carpets increases. The business activity in the margins overpowers the rest."

Shejal pats her on the head. She has obviously spent many hours poring over these figures to make sense of them.

"Even if you just put these little pieces together, it starts to tell a beautiful story all by itself. But you keep reading," says Neha as she gets up to leave, "little Jairam is about to grow up and get a life of his own."

"Ja, but he could have written about his shitty life as well. I still would have liked to read how he felt about it," says Shejal, still feeling disconnected from the diaries.

"Maybe he never told a story during this period because he felt like he had no life of his own, no story of his own to share just yet," says Neha with a shrug. "He wanted to build something different and better for his son, and your father wanted to build something better for his son, and you can now build something better and different for your son… or daughter," she is quick to add.

"Oh, God forbid," says Shejal, baulking at the prospect.

Janine drops her gaze, these stabs that he takes at the canvas on which she paints their joint future. "Ja, God forbid … you would make a terrible father," she lashes out, trying to cover a wound.

"You know, you're right … it's all so silly," says Shejal, lost in thought. "I mean, we all think we're special or breaking with tradition to do things for ourselves, but it's all just part of a pattern. A system of sameness that makes us think that we're all doing it differently."

He remembers the insidious and encoded rebellion of his university project, G(o)od Dog, and feels caught out, trapped in this web of repetition which leaves so little to be said for his originality.

"Oh Jairam," says Neha, as they take their usual walk around the neighbourhood, "it's such a beautiful evening."

Her brain is flooded with all the thoughts and theories she is trying to make sense of for her thesis. *Stop thinking, stop thinking,* she tells herself, envious of Jairam who moves through life one smell at a time.

The gentleness of the warm evening soon takes over, helping her to see the world outside. She has rarely taken time to notice the architecture of the houses, the colours of the roofs, the cars in the driveways.

"Oh," she sighs, letting his leash droop, "we have become people hiding in a fort and calling it paradise."

She stops. Her body cringes. It is a catcall. A whistle meant for whores or women who men deliberately choose to disrespect. She is the only one walking on the street. It must be intended for her. She hears the whistle again and the sound of a car approaching from behind.

"Hey, hey," says the voice, "don't walk away. We just want to say hello."

Neha turns on her heels. She is determined to nip this in the bud. She moves towards the dark blue Citi Golf with windows tinted an ominous black. She remembers walking past the car parked on the side of the road. She did not think anyone was inside it. The thought of those anonymous eyes on her all the while makes her shiver.

"Hello neighbour," says the boy. All the windows of the car roll down in sync, revealing four people in the car, all of whom are black, all of whom are smiling at her.

"Hello," she says sourly as she looks at the driver, but his impossibly boyish face makes her anger feel disproportionate.

"You stay on this road," he says more than he asks.

"Yes, I do."

"And you walk your dog right past us and you don't say hello."

"Your windows are so dark. I didn't see you." She gives a little laugh, imagining how ridiculous she must have looked from behind those black windows, engaging Jairam in conversation.

"We just come to this area," he says. "You the first person we see, otherwise there is only white, white, white … all boere here," he says, raising his friends to a chuckle.

"Oh, I know," says Neha, "yes, you will find that people are a bit unfriendly in this area."

"Uhm! Strue's Bob, we like to stand on the street to meet, talk to the neighbours, but eish … there is no one here," says one of the boys from the back whilst chewing on the end of a plastic straw. "In Soweto everyone stands on the streets, talking, drinking beer on Sunday. But here, everyone is locked up in the house."

They have a point, she thinks. "Ja, it's different from Lenz too."

"Ow, ekasi," the driver laughs. "You also understand that township life. It's our culture," he sings, sticking out his hand to make a gesture of affiliation.

"Ja, I guess so," she laughs. "Ekasi." She says it softly, trying the label on for herself.

The rest of the boys in the car whistle and hoot as if welcoming her into the fold.

"So, why did you leave Soweto?" she asks. "Why did you move here?"

"Eish…" he says, scratching his head as if wondering where to start his long list of reasons.

"Oh, never mind," she says, realising how difficult she finds it to answer this very question herself. She turns to leave.

"Ei, us, we must meet and keep in touch, you know, township style," he says. "I'm Kathlego. Wena?"

"Neha"

"Nay-hah," he repeats, then, "We lose people, we lose ourselves."

"Yes, yes, you're right." It will be nice to have neighbours to talk to for a change.

Silence: a lack, an absence of sound. But Neha can't decide what the difference is between its use in the expression of both peace and protest.

"Jairam, you bugger," she mumbles quietly in the university library, knowing that it is *his* diaries that force theory up into the air and then leave it there so that she is left with nothing solid to write a thesis about. It is his silences (for they seem to be multiple) that disrupt two ways of seeing: passive and active, disturbing and dormant, evident and completely blank. It is as if Jairam is some third thing, slipping past these two poles. *Is this a racial characteristic,* she wonders, *this ability, agility, to walk on tight ropes? The South African Indian, caught between worlds and at home in none? Being privileged enough to be able to write and hence to fight, yet stunted by political infancy and fear?*

The diaries, although written during a period of political chaos, are anything but political. And yet the political landscape interrupts Jairam's ideals of self-fashioning all the time. There are riots that force him to flee, conditions that lead him to compromise on where to buy his house and open his shop. Now that Shejal has finally gotten past volume four, he seems to think of this as apathy. But this label of "coward" is too easy for Neha. She knows that Jairam was always more than just one person at a time. How ironic that Jairam writes *"This is my silent self"* at the very beginning of volume six, the first of only two journals written in English, the ones that she and Shejal initially thought were fake.

> *I saw my mother reading my diary when I went to sit outside the*
> *shop. I have decided, then, to continue that one and leave it out*
> *on the counter as per usual for her amusement and as my decoy.*
> *And this one, my secret self, I will hide far away from prying eyes.*
> *I write in English, which she cannot understand – my secret self*
> *can remain as silent as a blank piece of paper.*

The secret and silent self happens to be Jairam's more verbose, insightful and witty one.

The diaries are arranged in a very curious manner; the first four seem to be written with the intention of keeping the shop accounts in order. It is only by the end of volume four, when he starts to sell carpets on the side, that words begin to creep into his world. By volume five he is well practiced in the art of journaling, one which he seems to have perfected unintentionally over time. In this volume he narrates his struggles with trying to establish a thriving carpet trade. He records his several difficult trips into the Transvaal in order to set up a network and to ascertain the feasibility of opening up his first shop there, instead of in Durban. He wanted to be far away from his family. He was afraid that they would force him to take over their general supplies store; a point which Shejal finds endlessly amusing since it resembles his own life so much.

Neha has also noticed that the less certain he feels about himself, the more he writes, as if he were relentlessly putting himself together in words on paper. Where is the silence and where is the song? Which is the absence and which the presence, she cannot say for sure.

To complicate matters further, about half-way through volume seven he realises:

> *My wife has taken over where my mother left off and she likes to read my diary too. Oh, though I must be a mystery to her as she is to me – we have only known each other for two short months now. I write, in the other diary, of who I think she would like me to be although I am not sure of who it is that she would like me to be. I can only hope to keep the fantasies of a young bride alive.*

In the dummy diaries he willingly becomes a ghost to himself as he writes for foreign eyes. He inscribes silly trivialities, sometimes religious scriptures or translates articles from an English newspaper into Gujarati just to fill the space. These dummy diaries are supposed to serve as a form of textual noise that distracts from his true self as it appears in the secret ones. Yet the secret diaries have their own tendency towards lyrical fantasies and whimsical dreams from time to time, making them no less fictional than the dummies. Neha therefore believes that Jairam made two silences (or two sounds) of himself.

For a moment, she looks about her, across the field of desks crowned with the hunched backs of students. There are parts of her body gone numb and her back hurts from the stiff wooden backrest. The fluorescent lights buzz overhead and the click of the librarian's mouse can be heard. *I am frigid and old*, thinks Neha, *frigid and old*. She sits amongst her many textbooks and uses them as company. Books, so many books, all of which have, over time, turned people into redundancies. Yet the little time that she has been spending with Kathlego and his boys recently has made her wish for company with more visceral dimensions. *If we lose people, we lose ourselves*, she thinks, repeating Kathlego's words. She slams hard against the library doors as she exits, as if pushing past a pair of tight, silent lips.

✳

They ruffle the duvet around their bodies and use it to prop up the books. Now that they have reached this point where the English and Gujarati diaries intersect, Shejal reads from the dummy diary and Janine from the silent self.

"You find it? 12 July 1938?" he asks so they can match the dates of the corresponding entries.

"Yup, got it."

"*Oh, how I love her heart, her warm smile. I feel blessed to be in the company of a wife such as her*," reads Shejal.

"Now let me tell you what he really thinks," says Janine, feeling the power of having the secret self to read.

I am a newly married man and a slow learner. But what I have learnt is that women, all women, like to be appreciated for things other than their bodies. It is not sufficient to say how much you worship her breasts or her naked back … this does not go down well. It is as if these creatures are above the comfort that another warm body can offer. It is the praise of her spirit that she best responds to and when I give her this and offer these compliments profusely, she becomes more willing to offer me her body without me having to feel as if I am stealing.

"Joh, brah, your ol' timer was a playa," she remarks.

"What can I say, we have a way with ladies," he smirks, reaching under the covers to grab her buttocks. "Oh, but wait, first I should tell you how special I think you are before I make a pass at you, right?"

"Well, if you mean it … it wouldn't hurt," she grumbles.

"Eish, let's just read." He turns the page. "Oh, it's Bhagavad Gita again, blah, blah, blah … and then … *I do not know if my wife would like to come to the shop with me. If she would, I hope she will make this request of me. I do not know if she is happy at home. If she is, I wish that she would make this known.*"

Janine takes over.

The only condition of my leaving was that I marry before I went to the Transvaal. I do not know if it is she who is to look after me or I who must look after her. The shop does not do so well. There are many expenses to cover and I do not know if I can provide well enough for the two of us. Our home is a miserable back room in Mr Patel's garden on the far end of Fietas. It is a sorry excuse for a house and I feel bad to leave her cooped up in there all day. But what else is there for her to do? She does not seem to mind much. Maybe she does not complain since she sees how dishevelled and pathetic I am when I come back home. When I look at my wife, I feel pity. I do not know if she is terrified of me at times, there is only meekness in her eyes.

"Joh! That doesn't sound like my grandmother!"

"Shut up," says Janine before she continues.

Women are such fragile things. I can only be respectful and exercise some gentleman's chivalry in front of her. Maybe it is the little gestures that will help since I have no power to make bigger ones like buy us a house of our own.

"Oh, that's so sweet," says Janine as she pouts.

Shejal recognises this expression that she wears whenever they watch a romantic comedy together. Her eyes are saying, "I wish I had a man like *that*."

Maybe she can, he thinks; *if Jairam can do it, so can I.*

December 2001

They have only one car between the two of them. As Govind drives her home from grocery shopping, she remembers how the idea of him driving her everywhere used to give her warm fuzzy feelings. How they used to coo, "Aw, you don't have to," and "No, I really want to" to one another. But now that they are married, it has ceased to be romantic in her mind. And he won't let her drive his car: "Woman just don't know how to treat a BMW."

With all the things needed for their new house, Kumari has had little option but to part with all of her savings. Now that they are done fitting the barbed wire, burglar bars, motion-sensor lights, infrared beams and a double gate on every door, all her money is gone – none left for a car of her own. She sighs as they pull into their driveway. Her heart laments her loss. *I bought a jail when I could have bought myself wings instead*, she thinks.

It is in the kitchen that Kumari feels most at home. Not the garden, the large bathroom, nor the entertainment rooms give her this supreme sense of ownership. Not even their bedroom excites her as much as the four cream walls of the kitchen do! She has already packed the new crockery twice. But today she starts again. She pulls out the classical white dinner set, lays it on the table, cleans out the cabinet with her bright orange dust cloth and even hums while doing so. She sprays the plates with scents of mint, lemon, orange and peach blossom and then finds a new order to put them back in again. *Now, now it works*, she thinks, imagining herself looking more elegant as she retrieves these dishes, her guests watching as she does so.

She turns the bottles of her complete collection of Robertson's spices so that all the labels face forward. It is only *she* who can tell you where to find the ground nutmeg (fourth bottle, second row) where the mayonnaise is (fridge, third row, at the back) or even where to find the cake-lifter (bottom drawer, on the right). It belongs to her. Govind does not know a thing about the kitchen. He called a spatula a "flipper" the other day, like it was some kind of dolphin. He does not even know how to sort dirty laundry and load the washing machine. Here he cannot even pretend. Here, she is the master. *The kitchen belongs to me and I to this kitchen*, thinks Kumari as she brings the black granite countertop to a shine in which she can see her own reflection smiling back at her.

"Fuck it!" screams Devon as he punches down the cushions on the sofas.

"Sjoe, what is this? Extreme cleaning?" quips Neha.

"I hate it when he asks to come over on the weekends," he moans.

"Oh, your *Ouen*," she giggles.

"Ja, and it's always the same old story, ugh."

"It's the holidays. It's a hard season to stay un-gay."

She quickly turns on her heels as she hears the doorbell ring. "Good luck."

"Hey, Owen," says Devon, opening the door. "Wow—late night?" The dark circles under the eyes give him away.

"Oh ja, we had our office party last night," he says, dropping his head to the ground in shame. "God, I'm just in the wrong bleddy industry to

reform." Owen bites his lip bitterly as if to draw his own blood. "God …
God," he pleads with the sky.

"Take a seat," says Devon, already knowing what to anticipate with
this vicious circle of sin, shame and repentance.

"I was with someone," he mumbles, on the verge of tears. "All this
time, it was just in my head, but now I don't know what kind of a
monster I am."

"Who were you with?" He is shamelessly reading into Owen's life as
if it belongs on the back pages of YOU magazine.

"God!" he exclaims again, sending a jolt through Devon. "My co-
worker brought a date. *His* date."

"Oh my," says Devon, stopping himself from grander expletives.

"I'm just in the wrong damn industry. I think I should quit my job."

"I mean, do you really think sacrificing your job is going to change
things for you?"

"No, but what else can I do now? Surely God will run out of forgive-
ness. I would if *I* was him."

"But you're not! There's something to be grateful for."

"I'd rather be a slave to God than be a slave to my body," he says
softly. "Because I only hurt myself that way and not other people …
Not my mother, or my father, or God, or my co-workers. It's just me
and that's okay – right? Christ suffered didn't he?" He tilts his head up,
slightly to the side.

Devon softens at the sight of his glance, of his desperate plea for
acceptance. "Christ suffered so you don't have to, you don't have to
crucify yourself like this every time. It's not healthy. Well, at least I don't
think it is."

Owen begins to cry, a few stray tears make dark spots on his smooth
velvet jacket. He soothes them away with his fingers as he tries to contain himself.

"Hey…" whispers Devon. It is unbearable to watch a man castrate himself in front of him. He strokes his back, getting caught in the soft brush of the velvet along his palm.

✳

"Oh, Captain," she starts as he catches her off guard with an early return.

"Hi, Janine, everything go okay?"

"Yup, Amy's still sleeping, of course."

"Yes, I didn't expect either of you to be up so early. I was hoping to sneak out for a round of golf." He walks to the kitchen. "Would you like some orange juice?"

She watches him fiddle with his blazer. Her eyes follow his fingers as they get lost between the gold buttons and navy-blue loops.

"Yes, sure … So you play golf?"

"It's the only hobby I have," he says sheepishly.

Janine wonders just how many someone is supposed to have.

"Do you like golf?" he asks.

"No, no. I don't play or watch, it seems boring."

"That's exactly what Amy says," he laughs.

She smiles, although annoyed at being compared to a 5-year old.

"So what do you do with your spare time?"

"Ah, nothing much," she answers, trying to find something substantial enough to count as a hobby. "I just hang out with my friends. So, you want me to stay here while you go play a game of golf?" She would rather probe into his life than have him probe into hers.

"No, I couldn't ask that of you. Besides, I have to get her back to her mother's. Amy has some birthday party or the other to go to."

"Oh yes, she told me about that."

"God, Christ! Her *mother*," he grits his teeth, already thinking of the inevitable encounter. "Why is it that women fight like that? They say things like, 'No I'm not angry,' even though you can see that they want to bite off your balls."

Janine is taken aback by the sudden change in tone, wondering where the congenial, laughing, smiling Captain flew off to.

"She can't stand the sight of me, that woman."

"Sjoe, what kind of a monster are you?" asks Janine before she thinks to restrain herself. She laughs to indicate that it was a joke.

"The kind that didn't pay enough attention to her," he sighs, sucking in his lips and popping them out again.

"You know, if you tell her what a good mother you think she is and that you appreciate her for how she handles Amy and stuff, I'm sure she'll come round."

"You think so?"

"I think so, Captain," she smiles shyly.

"Well, you know, I think you're right. And for Christ's sake, Janine, just call me Ben already!"

"Neha," says Shejal, "your friends are here to see you."

After shaking hands with everyone in the entourage, Shejal leaves the room. No one in the house, other than Neha, seems to be impressed with their company.

"Hey," says Neha as she comes up the passage. Having just woken up, she is still in her pyjamas.

Kathlego and his boys stroll in as if they have all suffered the same accident and all have the same limp in the right knee. They wear their usual uniform: baggy jeans, All-Star shirts and sneakers. The shortest boy, Sifiso, wears a spotty that hides most of his face.

They make themselves comfortable in the lounge. Sifiso scowls, clicks his tongue and shakes his head in disgust. "Hayi, man, sies," he fumes talking to no one in particular.

"What?" she asks amongst the murmur of clicking and cursing.

"You know, yesterday, the neighbours, they got robbed. TV, hi-fi, everything is gone from their home. And now this morning, they come asking us if we saw anything, if we know anything! Tsek!"

"So, maybe they just wanted to know if you saw anything."

"Hayi, sisi, please! It's cos we black. They won't ask you for anything else, won't ever knock on your door and won't even greet you in the street. It's cos we black. Now they think we know the crooks or we *are* the crooks, sies man –"

"I think you're being paranoid," says Neha as she takes a seat.

"You don't know how these people look at us in the street."

The group continues shaking their heads at the injustice they suffer.

"Ha, you laughing, Neha? I'm serious. These boere they just don't want us around," he says bitterly. "Ja, we don't have nice things like them, but it doesn't mean we want to steal it from them. They only know a black man in orange or blue overalls."

Kathlego makes several hand signals and one of his sidekicks disappears out the front door, returning a few moments later with a bottle of Black Label for everyone. He opens a quart and hands it to Neha. She sips it slowly – never having had one for breakfast before – and with a frothy fist, it punches her in the gut. They slowly calm down, reflecting on how unwelcome they feel in the area.

"This land will never belong to us black people! You and me, we aren't just visitors here in Alberton," Kathlego laments.

"You and me," she says softly. Neha marvels at the generosity with which he so easily includes her in the framework of blackness. He never bore any hostility towards her for being an Indian – an Indian who helped turn their mothers into maids and their fathers into garden boys. An Indian who has watched a man old enough to be his grandfather being murdered and left unnamed and unclaimed. She ruffles the short sprouting hairs on his head as she walks to the kitchen to throw some of the beer down the sink.

"It's just that us black people, we accept that we must struggle and must fight for our place in the world … hayi – I just want to take it all for granted," he says, dismissing the doctrine of suffering and progress with a heavy click of his tongue.

"Doesn't everyone?" she asks. "Aren't we all just struggling through life?"

"But we – the black people – go the extra mile, working like dogs in shit jobs for more hours than we have to, trying to move out of the townships. Struggling, struggling, struggling to just to prove we can be part of it all," he says. "And why?"

"Because we can't take it for granted," she whispers, finally seeing his point. She cocks her head up at him. Kathlego is a diamond in the rough. He is bold and clever with fiercely aggressive eyes in which the dangers of the world are kept alive.

"And now, Neha, when you look at me like that?" he asks.

She is lost in his eyes as if playing a seductive game with the swords she finds there.

"Oh it's all just boring you know," says Kumari as her friends probe into her life.

"It's been so long since we've seen you. You're even looking different," says Janine trying to make nothing more of her friend's weight gain.

The Five hover around Kumari as they soak in the details of their friend; the red dot in the middle of her forehead, the loose pants, sloppy T-shirt and a pair of fluffy green slippers that people wear in their own houses, not when they've come for a visit. Her hair, which is usually twisted into a tight, neat bun, sits lopsided at the back of her head.

"You look tired," says Neha.

"Ja, late night," she mumbles.

Although she is in no mood for conversation, they continue engaging her, trying to get her to answer just one question: "Are you pregnant?"

"Not sick or anything?" asks Devon.

"No! I'm fine, dammit."

"Shh!" says Shejal. He turns up the volume on the TV, wanting to catch snippets of Marike de Klerk's memorial service.

"Funny they don't show her apartheid triumphs," scoffs Neha.

"You know what they say, there's only good memories of the dead," says Kumari. Then she stands up. "Okay guys, thanks. Thanks for picking me up, but I need to get back home."

"It's no problem, Kumi, we keep telling you that, even if it's *every* week, just for a little bit … it's fine," says Shejal.

"No, no, don't be silly, I can't keep bothering you people."

They try to drag out the goodbye, each visit with Kumari feeling like the last.

January 2002

Owen surprises Devon in his shop one afternoon just before closing time.

"I know it's late, but I was just dying to tell you, and waiting for tonight wasn't an option," he says. His fingers anxiously knit together into a koeksister.

"Gosh, you look really nice today," says Devon to prompt him.

He's wearing a deep-stained denim blazer with a sky-blue shirt and well-fitted black pants. He even smells better than usual. And the downtrodden expression that is usually chiselled into his features has vanished, leaving him with bright eyes and a giddy smile.

"Ja, all dressed up today. It's a special day," says Owen as his jaw trembles. "Ey, man, it's hectic. I actually can't believe it's happening! God, I dunno – I think I'm in love."

"In love?"

"Well, I can't say for sure. But she actually said yes when I asked her out."

"What?"

"Yes, Luanne, from church, you know her, right? Tonight's our first date." He beams.

"Wow," says Devon, unable to respond to such an unexpected turn in the story.

"I'm so silly. Why didn't I think of it all this time? A girl was what I needed. My mother was right," he laughs.

The hair on the back of Devon's neck bristles. He does not think much of Luanne, but turning her into collateral damage seems especially cruel. He picks up a bottle of Windolene and fires it like a gun at the wide storefront window. He shines the glass furiously with a balled-up piece of newspaper, willing transparency back into a world plagued by destructive denialists.

✳

"Now I know what it's like to be Jairam," says Janine, yawning and stretching languidly as she wakes up from her fifth sleep that day. "Who gets sick like this during their holidays?" she gripes.

"Well, apparently you do," Shejal laughs as he fluffs up their pillows and tries to make his side of the bed a little neater. "So just stay there. I can get anything you need."

"God, I hate swallowing these antibiotics, they're as fat as bullets," she moans.

"Drink up and swallow," he says, standing over her with a glass of water.

He leans over and kisses her on the forehead – a calm balm for her hot skin. Shejal plays an efficient nurse. He opens the windows and picks up the stray dirty tissues that dot the room like snow. He also folds the laundry and puts it into the cupboards. *Who is this man?* she wonders as he places a steaming cup of lemon-flavoured Med-lemon on her bedside table without his usual need for praise.

"Do you feel like watching a movie or something?" asks Shejal. "I can bring my laptop here for you, if you like."

"No, no, I'm feeling more alive now. Do you wanna read some more of the diaries, or you not in the mood for that?'

"Okay, ja ... cool," says Shejal and he quickly brings out two volumes from under their bed.

"God, we're in the most exciting part ever," she exclaims as she remembers where they left off. Jairam soon tired of a lonely marriage and ended up taking a lover instead. Even Shejal is caught up in the intense romance, completely bypassing the dummy diary to just read the real drama as it unfolds.

"Okay, 2 February 1941," says Shejal, setting the tone.

To write in English bears a certain freedom for the soul. It is a freedom to become any man. It has just dawned on me that it would be impossible for me to put into words my current doings in my mother tongue. Nirupa soon tired of my diaries and I could easily switch back to Gujarati, but it is English that puts no judgement on my affairs and English that makes words that would seem so rude, now writeable. It feels liberating – picking parts off a woman and putting them on paper: buttocks, breasts, vagina ... I blush just looking at them on the page. And if I look back, it is in English that Kamala and I spoke our first words to each other. She is Tamil and apart from that, she knows only a little Hindi but no Gujarati. It is English that we both know! English! This was our humble beginning, a few words a day until words no longer sufficed. But we paved that road, English brick by English brick, until the concrete set and we tramped hard all over it with the weight of our bodies.

"Eish, gramps," says Janine.

"Oh please, we all think it, some just go the extra mile to write it. Next entry," he says, "5 February 1941."

Oh, this woman wraps cords around me! To use Bobby Khana's

expression, 'she's a killer diller!' To feel this flesh fold and wriggle
like an earthworm in the soft soil, it is only Bobby Khana's
expression that comes to mind – 'she's a killer diller!' The silly
fellow was only talking about the centrefold in a magazine at the
time – he does not know the full extent of his own phrase.

She intoxicates me. I worry that we are getting comfortable
and sloppy and will get caught. This morning I did not even lay
out the canvas sheeting on the carpets in the backroom before
I threw her on them! And we stayed a little too long and
Mr Govender was there waiting in the front when we entered
again. What pains I took to make up a story of the cleaning
instructions that I was giving Kamala so she could clean up the
very messy backroom.

"Remember how Neha was saying this is so much like our story," says
Janine thoughtfully. "She's right …"

"Oh please."

"Come on, dark girl of Tamil origin and sacred golden-brown roti-
boy who defile each other," she laughs.

"Hey, I didn't keep you locked up in a room, okay," he says, "though
that would be nice."

"Argh, Shej, can you get me that Vicks inhaler thing, please? My
nose is so clogged."

"Yup, sure where is it?" he asks feeling in the folds of the duvet for it.

Shejal likes this, this altruistic side of himself that is as infectious as
Janine's virus. He begins to see the truth behind his grandfather's words
that "a little bit of courtesy and kindness towards a woman has its own
rewards". Now that the role has turned into habit, he realises that being
kind to her is not something he does for her, but something he does for
himself. He strokes his hand across her smooth head, turning the soft
strands away from her face and over his fingers. By taking responsibility

for a human life other than his own, by seeing to her needs and desires, his impact on the world no longer seems abstract. It is the tangibility of her grateful smile that brings him back to himself. She kisses and strokes the back of his hand across her cheek as if it is made of the smoothest glass. There is love growing inside of him and it spreads through him with the clarity of a cure. She curls under the enticing caresses and not even the medicinal smells of eucalyptus and lemon can keep him from her.

Nights press the hardest. Devon works on his assignments. Shejal and Janine stay locked in their room. The TV is uninspiring and Neha's eyes gloss over from reading too much. She answers the quiet knock at the front door with excitement, knowing it can only be the guys. But she is surprised to find Kathlego alone. Glass bottles of beer clang together as he carries them in a Shoprite bag. He looks frail and delicate without his band of brothers around him. There is softness about him that Neha has never seen before.

"Eish," he whispers, stubbing his toe on the skirting.

"Are you drunk already?"

"What are you saying? It's too early to be drunk," he bellows drunkenly.

"My room," she whispers. "Don't wanna wake everyone."

His bouncy limp has evolved into a calmer stroll as he tries to keep himself moving forward towards the shred of light at the end of the passage.

"Sjoe, bright walls," he comments, never having been in her room before.

"Ja, it was a moment of inspiration that passed too soon."

"There you go, Neha," he says grandly, opening a beer for her.

They sit on the bed and his life begins to pour out of him – how he feels compelled to send money to his grandmother to help feed his sister's children, how he gets treated like an idiot at work, how all of his friends just want to get rich and be happy, how the alignment on his car is shot and the clutch pad needs to be changed.

Neha drinks to catch up. She wants this fountain of woe to pour out of her as freely as it does from him, thinking that if her heart were to break like a dam wall then she could escape the drudgery of it all. Yet all she feels is her body growing heavy and her tongue growing thick from the beer.

"Hayi, sisi, you falling asleep there. I rather go," says Kathlego getting up.

"No, no, no," she whines, jumping up to stop him from leaving.

As she swings past him to block his path, his hand brushes against her bum. He leaves it there without a word. She turns back to look, and the fire, the rough heat in his eyes draws her in. All the hairs on her body stand up. She can smell the lotion on his neck. It is here that she kisses him first as he squeezes all the soft bits of flesh that he can find on her body. All of this is a prelude to the moment when they hopelessly and clumsily fall to the bed, together.

Kumari wakes up in a sweat, feeling for each of her limbs in turn. In her dream she was paralyzed. She stares at the red, luminous digits on the clock: 22:20. At night the area becomes so still that even the whistle of the trees in the backyard spooks her. With all this space for the two of them there is much room for emptiness.

She remembers the house she shared with the rest of the Five. The rush of the steady stream of water and the smell of Sunlight bubbles as Janine washes the dishes, the high pitched screams of Neha chasing after the dog, Devon trying for solemnity as he lights candles all over the house before he moves into his time of prayer, and Shejal clicking the mouse and bragging about his computer game virtuosity. All at the same time, all of that noise and life. And all of it happening without her. Her life, she now sees, exists in separate episodes to theirs.

She rings and listens to Govind's droll voicemail. He does not like to be disturbed when he is working overtime. He is eager for his promotion and spends many nights at work. She fulfils her duty in supporting his dreams, as he will hers – when he is less stressed, more settled in his career. Patience is a virtue, as her mother always says. She cradles the soft flesh of her abdomen and nurses its gentle yearning. She is already caught in the conversation that extends from her navel; little, loving voices that bathe her in quiet joy. She must, as she does every night, turn them away kindly. She must wait for Govind to give time and then seed to her dreams.

FIRE

April 2002

Janine sinks into the bath. She is held underneath by the weight of the result – positive, all three of them. Positive. She knows she should have extended the investigation to at least five. Now that she is all out of pretty pink sticks on which to draw more pretty pink lines with her own urine, she freezes like a corpse and sinks further and further into the hot tub. *Maybe my heart will exhaust itself and I won't have to deal with this,* she thinks, feeling her pulse beat at a frenetic pace in the boiling water. *How is it that when life seemed to be going so right, it has actually been going so wrong?*

She sucks in her breath and drops under the water, coming up again with a face full of tears that are not her own. She's still numb from the shock. She feels around her stomach, the hard bones of her pelvis, the slope of her abdomen and the small quiet space between her legs. *There is no space for this baby here,* she thinks. *Shejal will stop loving me and start resenting me. I will stop loving and start resenting this baby.* The storyline floods her mind as she remembers how it was that she came into being.

"Dear Baby," she says formally as she puts a hand on her tummy, "I will spare you hell. I will spare you poverty and I will spare you from a lack of love, because there is never enough to go around in this world."

She closes her eyes and listens to this truth infiltrate her body. She imagines the pin-sized life inside of her, listening, agreeing and turning back to the light from which it was born.

"You okay in there?" Neha's muffled voice comes from behind the door. "You've been in there for like two hours."

Janine can hear Jairam's anxious sniffing at the base of the door.

"I'm fine," she says. "Fine – just pregnant."

"Fuck me! Fuck me! Let me in!" shouts Neha.

"It's open," says Janine, and Neha storms in.

She stares. Her big eyes expand at the realisation of ripeness in her friend's body.

"I'm getting rid of it." In the face of Neha's shock, her own suddenly seems insignificant and she finds it in herself to shrug at her own suggestion. "And not a word to Shejal, he doesn't need to know," she adds.

Neha pushes the pretty pink sticks off the toilet seat and sits down, "Are you sure? About not saying anything before…"

They both stare down at her belly and watch her skin morph under the dancing ripples of water.

"Not a word Neha, not a word! Now's the time to keep a secret of mine just as well as you did Shejal's."

"Okay, but …" says Neha, growing teary. "I'm sorry," she whimpers and runs out, ashamed that she cannot be brave at a time like this. "What have I done, what have I done?" she murmurs as she flees. "Why did I give them Jairam's diaries?"

She saw the way in which Shejal picked up habits from his grandfather. She even joked that she would buy him a pocket watch, a pipe and a pair of black-rimmed spectacles. But this is too much, too much of history coming to life! It is too late to take back the past now.

✳

"Sjoe! Maybe it will wake me up a bit," says Peter as he takes his cup of coffee from Devon's hand. He arches his back like a cat as he breathes in the heady aroma. They munch biscuits while they wait for further studying inspiration to return, but by the time they finish their coffee, none has come.

"You know, Pete, there is something I've been meaning to ask you," says Devon. "You remember how you said that you thought Owen was gay? Well, I was just wondering that if he was – what kind of counselling am I expected to give him … if he's gay?"

"Well, I dunno, celibacy?"

"But, I mean, we don't expect that of other parishioners, so why him?"

"Ja, but it's not like we can marry him to another man before God, like you can a man and a woman."

"So, he would just have to accept half a life then?"

"Well, it's a sacrifice like any other, I guess. Everyone has a weakness to sacrifice if they want a relationship with God."

"But is it really okay, I mean, to call gayness a weakness?"

"Jirre man, Devs, I dunno. What is all this about? Did he come back telling you he is gay? Eish, that Luanne must be one hectic chick if she could put him in reverse gear like that."

"It's not a reverse gear, it's not backward or sinful or weakness."

"Sjoe, okay. I didn't mean to sound offensive. Hey – you and I both live holy, celibate lives, so why shouldn't someone else who wants a relationship with God do the same?"

Devon sighs. As if it is as simple as that. Peter can go on to fall in love, marry and have children if he wants, whereas Devon and people like Owen will forever be stuck. Sick of all the quietism and evasiveness, he feels himself reeling for a fight, but without a clue about where to throw the first punch.

✳

Janine's knuckles dig in with the strength of a pitchfork as she kneads the dough. Her hands, now covered in flour, are corpse-grey. They work with the mechanical method of a zombie, running off the memory of the many rotis she has made in her life. She sweats from her labour. The stray hairs on her forehead stick to her head and turn into slick, black rivers as they meander down her temples.

"Do you want some help?" asks Neha, witnessing the thrashing, burning and grunting.

"No, no. I can handle this." She pulls her slouching back stiff as she continues.

Now making little balls, Janine stops and draws back. She awakens to the horror of her own hands. It becomes too difficult to pull at the generous whole of unformed dough and reduce it to small parts. The squealing as it is made to stretch and string from the force of her fingers is haunting. Neha hesitantly steps in and pats the balls into flat dots on the board and adds more flour before she begins to roll.

"Just leave it, will you?" snaps Janine. "If you don't make these properly, they won't come out perfectly round! See? There! Perfect!" she exclaims with aggression as she rolls out one in a flash and throws it on the hot tawa.

Neha begins to sob. The dark stench of death and sorrow collides with the promising smell of melting butter and roasting dough. It is too much of a contrast for her to handle. It is as if the dualities of the world have come into the kitchen to fight; death and food, sadness and warmth, sickness and nurturing.

"You should really start smoking," says Janine as she watches Neha crumble in front of her. "You will cry less." She drops the rolling pin and hands her the pack of cigarettes that she always carries on her. "Go on, get out!" she shouts, dismissing Neha from the room.

Alone, she falls back into the motion. She irons out the seams and brings each roti to its circular perfection. She pulls the first one off the tawa and, according to her own tradition, eats it herself. As the heat lathers her tongue, it sews up pieces of her broken soul.

"Joh! Check how you chowing that roti," exclaims Devon, catching her with her cheeks as fat as a hamster's. "Joh," he says again as he looks around the kitchen. There are unfried rotis everywhere; circular discs on the rolling board, on the kitchen table and the counters. There seem to be at least three times the usual amount.

"Who are you making all these rotis for? Who else have we got to feed?" he asks jovially.

"Fuck you!" she screams and flings one at him like a frisbee, but too limp to fly, it lands on the floor.

"Oh, Kathlego, *please*," says Neha as she hears his new plan for vengeance.

He is still angry at the slight that the Afrikaans neighbours made against him and his friends with regard to the burglary. He has been concocting plan after plan for retribution. He is careful, always, to run his latest strategy past Neha to gauge its viability. Once he started on a high note of actually hiring thieves to break into the house, but he has now toned it down to throwing toilet paper all over their roof or getting Jairam to shit on paper, which he will then place on their front doorstep.

"Let it be, live your life, man," she says.

"Nothing," he says dismally, "this is nothing to you. And to the white people also. They don't have to feel guilty, neh? But this is not nothing to me, Neha. They must feel guilty for the way they treat me and my friends. You think these people are your neighbours, but they are not thinking of you as a neighbour." He goes on like a broken record, "It is only once there is guilt that I will stop being angry."

Neha is certain that she can quote this verbatim by now.

"*You*, you can break the cycle," she says pleadingly. "How silly to wait around for white guilt … all this talk takes us nowhere! *Do* something, take action, take control, Kathlego."

"You know, you're right! We should do something. Meet me outside at eleven tonight," he says before he leaves.

The water gushes and drums against the bath tub, playing out the tune of hot anxiety that boils inside her. She pulls off her clothes and sits on the narrow edge of the tub. Shejal calls for her until he tires and gives up. She grasps the old paring knife and now, as she resurrects it from its jewellery box grave, the past comes along with it; her mother, her father, the seething pain, the angry sore – it flows through her veins like an infection, yellow, pussy and oozing. *It is them who poisoned my womb and aborted my baby!* The cold bite of the steel wings that kept her legs apart and the roughness of the white paper gown – she only saw *their* faces. She saw their wide-open lips and heard the sound of their ripping guffaws as they watched her at her most vulnerable; flat on her back with a tube stuck between her thighs. Not the nurses or Neha's brittle chatter could distract her from the pain and the black ghosts floating around the room, waiting to fill the space that the foetus left behind.

She holds the cold blade close to her flesh and presses down. Her hands begin to tremble. They have lost the steadiness of practice. Impulsively, she rips her skin and blood spurts like heavy teardrops weighted with her emotion. She closes her eyes, the sorrow and dirt ebbs out to the beat of her pulse. She climbs into the tub and the water is furiously hot. It sticks needles into her skin. Her fingers cling to the steel handles. She is determined to sit through this. She feels herself go up in flames. It is this very fire that purifies her. The heat penetrates deeper as it cleanses her blood.

She stands outside at ten minutes to eleven feeling energised by Kathlego's mystery plan. She spots him hovering further down the street and he waves her down. She runs along the quiet street to meet him. His hands are tucked inside the huge pockets of his hoodie. He quickly reveals a can of spray paint. He says nothing, but begins to smile as he shakes the can. She watches calmly as he paints big red letters on the neighbours' precast walls. The smell of damp spray paint makes her giddy. She is amused by her role as accomplice in this stupid and ineffective act of revenge, but if it brings Kathlego the closure he needs, she sees no harm in it.

"Your turn," he says handing the can over to her.

Neha stands for a while, trying to think of a suitable blood-red insult to paint next to Kathlego's "RACIST".

"RACIST Neighbour," laughs Kathlego as he sees her word develop next to his.

Neha smiles; this is the first time he has taken to her sense of irony. Once she is done, she quickly grabs hold of him, the rush of adrenalin feeling so much like love.

"Oh my God, there you are! I've finally got you! Red-handed!" a voice booms in the distance.

"Shit," says Neha as she turns, "quick, back to my place!"

They run, but are already being pursued. She cannot shut the front gate in time and they stop in the yard, resolved to face what they must.

"You!" The man in front of them has an intimidating frame. He steps closer to Kathlego, sticking his fat pink finger in front of his face like an imaginary gun.

"Mrs Erasmus told me to keep an eye on you and I was just waiting for you to get up to some shit so that I could take you off our streets."

"Pff," laughs Neha, "what are you, a cop?"

"Yes, and my name's Captain Viljoen," he booms. "Goes to show, hey?

You never know who your neighbours really are." He grabs Kathlego's hands. "Come with me."

Kathlego is dead silent. Neha can feel him quivering.

"Wait a minute," she says, stepping in front of Kathlego, "you can't arrest him! It was me. I did it. Look," she adds, presenting the can that is still in her possession. She offers a smile, feeling pleased to display this piece of incriminating evidence. "Even you saw *me* do it, not *him*. Kathlego just came along for company and kept warning me that I would get into trouble."

The captain eyes her suspiciously. He has no way of refuting her claim.

"Guh, what would I want to arrest a stupid teenage girl for?"

"Come on, you wanted to arrest someone didn't you, so here you are!" she shouts, sticking out her bony wrists, angry at the insinuation that she is not to be taken seriously as a threat. "You wanted justice, didn't you?"

"Oh, you children of today. I'll just tell Mrs Erasmus that you will paint her wall, which you *will* do." The captain sighs, disappointed. This is like scolding his daughter for being tardy with her domestic chores.

"But you!" he says regaining his composure and pointing past Neha at Kathlego, "I have my eye on you."

They stand still as the captain leaves. They wait a long minute before they turn towards each other.

"This was *my* fight," he says finally, seeing how she took possession of the whole affair.

"Oh, come on, any punishment you got would have been way worse than mine."

"You tell me to take action and then you turn the whole thing into a stupid joke."

"Did you really want to spend the night in jail? No, I didn't think so," she says, speaking into his silence.

"But I also didn't need you to save me!" he yells, walking away from her.

*

Her nagging always sets him off. She knows this much by now. And now the handle on the drawer is broken. It admonishes her with its cracked face, as if someone has pulled its nose right off. When did she develop such a harsh, judgemental eye with regard to her husband and become unable to hold her tongue about his deficiencies? She never saw herself as short in her pronouncements of others, but perhaps marriage does redefine you – in her case, poorly – as people so often say. She is failing at her role. And now the handle is broken – the dull bruise on her lower back is hidden and she writes it off as collateral damage – but everyone can see the state of her marriage from the drawer that has lost its neat symmetry. To further remedy the guilt, Kumari relies on the potent alchemy of love: his bitterness she exchanges for insecurity, his neglect for stress, and his shove for an embrace.

June 2002

Janine sings as she pops out of the bathroom. Her skin is fresh and shiny from her new ritual of a night-time bath. Shejal watches her lather on thick lotion with gentle ease. He feels pleased – finally the dark cloud that was visiting her seems to have lifted. He does not know what it was or where it came from – he never does – but he notices the usual signs that indicate its departure. She pulls on a pair of flannel pyjamas and climbs on the bed next to him.

"Okay, ready," she says, rubbing the last of the lotion into her hands.

He knows better than to touch her. She will come back to him when her heart is done with its dark business.

"So, where were we?" he asks as he thumbs through the diary, "Yes, here … 23 September 1943."

My son is growing into a young scamp, always behind his mother! I think it would do him good to spend some time in the world of men. But I cannot take him to work with me, although my wife suggests this too. I agree, and yet selfishness takes over. I would not be able to see Kamala with my son running around the shop. 'Let him stay at home until he is ready for school,' is what I said and earned myself a very poor veg curry and a watery dhal in return.

212

"Here, let me take over," Janine offers and begins to read. "24 September 1943."

> *Kamala has not come for two days now. But this is good, perhaps,*
> *scattering things out. 'How often do your front windows need to*
> *be cleaned?' asked Pen-knife Bobby the other day as he walked*
> *past my shop in his slick suit and shiny shoes … People notice*
> *these things and it is best to be vigilant.*

"26 September 1943," reads Shejal.

> *What a blow to my heart. Kamala came this morning, looking*
> *like one of those sad rags that sit in the bottom of her bucket.*
> *She is pregnant.*

"Oh God, this is horrible," says Shejal.

> *And she says the baby is mine. We sat in the dark of the backroom*
> *as she cried her heart out. And we decided now that there is little left to*
> *do but for her to visit that nurse who lives in Uncle Chunky's backyard.*
> *It is too horrible for me to write down the word, even in English.*

Shejal puts the diary down on his lap to digest the last entry. "God – this is hectic shit."
Janine blinks at him, slow and then fast, like a dumb bird. She says nothing but picks up the diary to read the next entry.

> *2 October 1943*
>
> *I have been suffering and losing sleep. Today she finally came*
> *back. She looks distraught and I don't think I will ever forgive*

myself for bringing this upon her. But we had no options, neither
of us would be better off if we had this baby.

She reads shakily. Shejal, too, bows his head in shame.

4 October 1943

I have the feeling she is avoiding me. I wonder if I bring back the
fear of having to face again all the horrible things she suffered?
Perhaps I must let her go. I cannot expect her to continue this
affair. It is unfair to her. I will get over it and continue to live as
one is expected to – decently and, above all, dutifully.

"This is so tragic," says Shejal, feeling the full impact of his grandfather's
loss. It is only because of this warm flourishing of empathy that Shejal
sees his grandfather as something other than the great family man and
the carpet salesman. He is not the monolith his grandmother made
him out to be, but a collection of greys and beiges that allowed for love
and its inevitable mistakes.

Janine sits silently next to him. Her body retracts in a desire to grow
smaller and eventually disappear.

"Your turn," says Shejal, handing the diary back to her.

She clears her throat before she reads.

14 October 1943

I had a dream. I saw my child… a broken foetus sitting at the
bottom of Kamala's bucket and Kamala sits on the side, crying on
her own. I hate my life. I hate myself.

She thrusts the book back at Shejal.

20 October 1943

Another dream: Kamala, me and the baby – alive and happy!
We have smiles on our faces and laughter fills the room. I woke up
miserable and, writing this, I still feel so hollow inside.

Shejal sees Janine all choked up by the tragedy and thinks it his duty to provide some rational comfort. "It was a crime of necessity. As harsh as it is, it had to happen this way," he whispers into her ear.

"Then you can forgive it?"

"Yes, of course."

"You can forgive it."

"Yes, yes."

"I had an abortion."

It is a long minute before he spins her around for answers. Her head remains stiff and bent forward.

"A crime of necessity, you said it yourself and you said it was forgivable," she whimpers from behind her black curtain of hair.

Suddenly, he begins to roar, "Fuck you! How dare you compare my grandfather's situation to ours?"

"Because we are in no position to have a child!" she yells, fuelled by his rage.

"Oh really – why? Do we both have some other family to feed? Fuck! Fuck! When? Why? Why? And you never said a word to me—"

"I *helped* you. I helped you, you son of a bitch!" she spits out, her hair flying wildly as she jerks her body around.

"You're an evil woman, Janine … You helped me? How? To walk around with my grandfather's guilt for the rest of my life? You didn't even give me a fucken choice!"

"Exactly, so you can tell yourself that for the rest of your bleddy life and feel pleased about it. You can feel as self-righteous as you want because you didn't have a choice. You need me to do your dirty work, Shejal, pick up your dirty fucken clothes, cook your food and then fuck you and abort the baby – you need me to take care of all the shit!"

Months and months of grunting labour on her back and Kumari has no result to report. The doctor said that everything is fine, that she is just too stressed to conceive. Why are the little voices rejecting her? Did she take too long to heed their call? Yet, the more she thinks about not stressing, the more stressed she feels. Does this doctor not know that she goes into battle every time to seek out her child?

As she lies beneath Govind – for it is an optimal time that cannot be wasted – she tries to release the sense of mission from her being. She finds it impossible that such fragile labour comes from the act of sex. Yet this impossible fact restores a new sense of hope in her, that violence can be turned into love. This baby, she knows, will recover Govind's tenderness. She imagines her insides to be like the downing in her duvet. She breathes deeply into her womb, aerating her soft-bed uterus. She even toys with the idea of looking for pleasure in the act of sex, but is distracted by the pastel shades of early life – its soft, vulnerable pink, its angelic white and its delicate, membranous grey.

"Come, come," she says softly to his seed as he climaxes. She waits for pollen to touch filament, for love to touch life. She falls asleep with her hands resting on her belly and her pelvis pointing skyward.

The doorbell rings late at night and Devon jumps up from the couch with fright.

"Owen?" he says, opening the door just a crack.

The mousy face lifts up. Devon has no choice but to let him in.

"I'm sorry. I know it's late and I know I should have called," he says. "Luanne and I had a date tonight and she tried to, you know, take things further, and I don't know what is wrong with me. I mean … I knew it was coming and I really psyched myself up for it and then I just couldn't handle it."

Devon sighs. He has had more than enough to deal with today. "You know, Owen, have you ever thought about being celibate?"

"What? And live like … what? A monk? You want me to walk around in one of those dull brown robes you wear during the Sunday services? I'm not some asexual zombie man." He shivers with disgust.

Devon drops his head, an asexual zombie of a man, is this him? Has he granted celibacy a false sense of dignity in his head? A way to simply avoid the messy business of being alive? Suddenly enraged by feelings of his own cowardice and shame, Devon changes course.

"You know what," he says, "forget what I just said, I think you should go on and be gay already! Ja, you heard me, go be gay! Go be as gay as a lark, my friend, like a fairy in a forest. Go! Because you know what, let me share a little secret with you. You think God's going to punish you? He won't, I promise you. He'll be angrier if you fuck up some girl's life because you wanted to marry her to cure yourself!" he booms. "And furthermore, you can't cure yourself. You just can't!"

Owen stands there nervously, on the verge of flight.

"You and me, we both make different kinds of idiots of ourselves," says Devon close to Owen's ear. He grabs him by the jaw and kisses him, long and hard, as if sucking out the very demon from him.

"What are you doing?" asks Owen as he wrestles out of his grip. "You fucken mad? You arsehole. Fuck you, you piece of shit! You're a monster," he shouts, running for the door.

Devon stands in the middle of the room. Half-alive to his reality, he calmly walks over to switch off the TV. His mind is a dense cloud, his body is warm with the heaviness of stored water and, like rain, he drops on the couch, almost peacefully.

Neha remains hunched over the kitchen counter drinking a beer, recovering from her last bout of neighbourly fence painting. She listens with a diplomatic ear despite the fact that these are probably her favourite three words in the whole wide world.

"You were right," says Kathlego, clutching his spottie between his palms as a sign of humility.

For Neha, these words hold more affective power than 'I love you'.

"It would have been hell if I got arrested that night. You did me a favour. You kept me out of big kak."

This is even better than she thought. She expected some resistance that would turn into a point of argument when he came skulking back. She muses over the power of influence she has over him. His openness to take advice from her fills her, in turn, with generosity, maybe even love.

"You see me, Neha. I am not invisible to you."

She drops her analytical stance and reaches for the base of his neck. She plants a gentle kiss on the slope, like mist edging the base of a black, graceful mountain.

Devon takes special care to prepare their Sunday lunch. He is determined to have stability amidst his chaos. The delicate attentiveness that cooking requires helps him to defuse the waves of anger and shame that made it impossible for him to return to church this morning. He has stepped out of a world with clear definition and no longer knows what truly counts as the right action. He slivers the fresh coriander with a chopping knife to add the last garnishing touch to his curry. Neha strains the rice through a colander in the sink and Shejal does his best to mash up the dhal just as Devon has instructed.

"Hey guys," says Janine as she enters timidly. "I have good news!"

"What?" Devon asks dully.

"Ah! The captain," she sings as she bats her eyelashes. She is teasing them with her story, letting only bits trail out of her mouth at a time. "Oh, he asked me to move in with him," she says in a breathy tone.

"What!?" Neha shrieks.

"Oh ja," she laughs, "not like *that*, of course. He asked me to be Amy's full-time nanny and I said yes."

Neha and Devon stare blankly at each other, wondering if it is necessary for them to live with this drama. An official break-up; Shejal has moved into Kumari's room, and although he and Janine sometimes scream at one another, they are no longer on speaking terms. Yet they are happy to pretend as if everything is alright, which is the most miserable part of it all. Shejal uses his easy escape route, evaporating into endless hours of TV and computer games. Janine, on the other hand, has become loud and boisterous. It is as if she is playing a big shiny brass instrument whose keys she cannot understand. She takes pains to show that she is reinventing her life. The grief keeps her on her toes as much as it keeps Shejal dead static.

"But, hang on, I thought that kid stays with her mother," says Devon.

"Oh well, now she is going with her boyfriend to Australia to check out the job prospects, so Amy is staying with her father from now on."

"But what about the day care, I thought you loved it at Never Never Land?" asks Neha.

"Well. You love it, you leave it," she says coldly, glaring at Shejal. "We all have to grow up at some point. And besides, I get free board and lodging at his house. I would be stupid not to take it."

"Great, we'll have to shoulder more expenses, but it seems worth it!" says Shejal, who has been left gritting his teeth for too long.

"So what then? Must I stay here, stuck with having you in my face all the time?"

"That's enough," Devon moans as he sees Shejal stand up to retaliate. "This is enough. I mean, maybe this is a good thing. We can't live like this anymore. It's just barbaric."

August 2002

At first it is uncomfortable to share a living space with strangers. There are many things that keep Janine creeping around the house like a stray cat because she has entered a world where everyone seems to have the lives depicted in glossy magazines. Today, though, she feels as if she has turned an invisible corner and the morning seems to unfold seamlessly before her. The security guard who controls the residential boom gate finally gives her a wave of recognition in return as she drives out to do some grocery shopping.

She zips into Sandton City, happy to know the exact quantities and varieties of food to buy. She is still enthralled by the privilege of shopping during off-peak hours. Now she can enjoy the freshest fruit and vegetables and clear checkout lanes along with the other leisurely housewives, while other people are pinned to their desks and mundane jobs. As she turns the corner, a lady stands in front of the refrigerator and minces her glossy pink lips as she decides on which concentration of orange juice to buy. She is one of those ladies who have their days to themselves while their husbands are at work and their children at school, who have time to apply their make-up and go to art classes, who can walk through the mall with a credit card and a pair of large black sunglasses perched on their heads like a makeshift Alice-band. Janine stretches across her to pick up a blend that she knows the captain enjoys. The lady looks up and gives her a gentle nod and then a smile. Janine grins at this acknowledgement. Carried away by a fantasy, she rises to the part of the captain's wife.

"Oh, my husband just loves this blend," she says.

"Well, I might as well give it a try then." The lady uses her manicured hand to take a bottle of the same from the refrigerator shelf.

"Have a good day," sings Janine as she pushes her cart forward.

"Thanks, you too," chirps the lady, pleased to have encountered a woman who understands the true complexity of picking out juice for her family.

When Janine left, it was him and his grandfather who mourned the loss of their respective lovers together. Shejal nears the end of volume ten and slowly, much to their mutual relief, the woman fades from Jairam's preoccupations, although the entries grow ridiculously thin.

12 November 1947

Who is this 'I', this person I look at in the mirror? And how many times must 'I' divide it? Son of, husband of, owner of …

Insipid and endless lamentations of his responsibilities, every one of which seemed to have been a burden. Shejal turns to the end of the volume, unable to take more of these depressing anecdotes.

"Neha!" he calls. There is an odd translator's note that he cannot make any sense of.

"What?" She pops her head around the door.

"Uh, I just want to know what 'frail hand' means. Here, under 23 June 1950."

"Oh, well, if you look at the original, the writing is all in a frail hand.

Sometimes Meela struggled to read it because it got so weak in places, especially towards the end … Look at the original, you'll see," she says. "We were wondering if he was struck by an early case of arthritis or something. I was waiting for you to reach there before I asked you."

"I don't know. So these entries were hard to translate?"

"Well, ja – but then if you look at the contents of this last volume…"

Shejal scans through the last pages and sees something familiar developing. Inventory lists and figures compiled in a scattered fashion.

"He ends where he starts," says Neha.

"So that's it?"

"I guess so. Now you can start your own story, instead of being cooped up with those diaries all the time."

Her room is different – everything is tidy and in its place. This is by no means her own doing; she has never mastered the art of organisation. Kathlego has dared to rummage through her mess and Neha musters an appreciable smile as he gestures towards the new bookshelf. He has spent the entire day assembling it from scratch. She watches as he unpacks her books, carefully aligning them in alphabetical order according to the author's surname. She has no heart to tell him that she prefers an arrangement according to genre and gives him a kiss, answering the need for appreciation imprinted in his eyes.

He has long since left his friends behind, choosing her company instead. He sometimes lights candles for lovemaking and is always careful to leave behind a flower, a chocolate or a note when he departs. They are horrible clichés that sometimes make her squirm, but he is a man in search, in service, of her heart. The weight of this responsibility makes her pensive. She is touched that she can inspire such change, such love, but can she really provide all of its meaning? If she were to harbour delusions of being his god, or his sovereign entity, she would lose every right to be imperfectly human and perfectly free.

✳

"It's me! Let me in already," says the squeaky voice, ridden with anxiety to get off the street and into the house.

More curious than upset, Devon opens the door and lets Owen in. "What the hell are you doing here?"

Owen struts in the house in his tailored blazer, a magnificent patchwork ensemble of different fabrics and colours.

"Oh, I call it my technicolour dreamcoat," he says as he catches Devon staring at him.

"It's lovely," says Devon, envious that he can pull off something as flamboyant as that.

"How have you been? *Where* have you been?" asks Owen. "I waited for weeks and then months for you to come back to church. And today I was certain that I would see you at Peter's ordination, but you weren't there!"

"Yes, yes," mutters Devon, all too aware that today was Peter's special day. It would have been the day of his ordination as deacon too. Despite wanting to go to support his friend, he could not find it in himself to face him or Father Robert.

"Why aren't you back at church?" he asks again, dropping all pleasantries. "Why haven't you returned? Why have you changed your cell number?"

"I thought you never wanted to see me again ... that you were gonna rat me out to Father Robert."

"Oh, you know *me* ... your average queen riding on a yo-yo," he says coyly. "I had an anger phase, then a binge phase, then a disgust phase and then I came to the reconciliation phase, but you weren't there. And I waited for you, but you didn't return … I got worried."

"Sorry to disappoint you. I am a fraud. I don't think I am coming back."

"What? Why not? You were the only person I could really talk to!" He sits down on the couch and bites his nails.

"Oh, stop that, will you?" moans Devon.

"You were the only person I could share my problems with without feeling judged, and then you would pray for me. I don't have many friends in Joburg. You were a real friend. I could tell you anything and you would still love me."

The fact that he has touched someone's life releases tenderness in him and he strokes Owen's brow with the tips of his fingers.

"In the church, everyone knows you gay," says Owen, "but they keep so silent about it that you don't know what's right or wrong anymore. They neither kick you out nor do they tell you it's 100 percent okay and invite you to please stay. They give straight people a list of bleddy commandments and an entire history of canon law, but you?" he snorts. "Just left wondering whether you're the work of the devil or not."

"I know, I know," says Devon. He sees the nuances of confusion float up in Owen's eyes and imagines that his must look much the same.

"That silence, it kills me. I can't take the silence. Maybe they want to kill me off with it."

"Yup, you're only allowed a backdoor entrance," says Devon as he reflects on the double bind they are in.

Owen chuckles at the innuendo and picks up Devon's hand to hold it between his. They sit there, locked in an earnest assessment of each other's eyes as they wonder what to do about *this*.

Devon can feel himself finally discarding the regal robes that have been weighing him down all this time. He decides to live nakedly and vulnerably in the dust of his uncertainty. When Owen kisses him, he does not resist but enters a world that he has denied himself for so long. He longingly pulls off Owen's mesmerising coat, eager to evoke its magic.

✳

The light falls differently on her face this morning and she stirs uncomfortably in bed. The intermingling of dream-time and reality disorients Janine. The captain came home scratching his head where the band of his cap had hugged it and started complaining about his ex-wife. She is happy in Australia, convinced that it is the right country for her to start a new life in. Last night was the night she got engaged to her boyfriend and the captain wore a different mask; furious, red, raging and above all passionate. Janine reached across the table to stroke his arm. Then he kissed her. He kissed *her* – this she is sure about … how strange it felt, a man cursing one woman and fucking another. Both she and the captain, giving comfort to one another, with different people stowed away in the backs of their minds. *Maybe we do belong together after all,* she thinks.

October 2002

"Oh, my depressed lover, fall into my arms," says Owen dramatically.

"I'm not depressed," Devon mumbles into his shoulder.

"Of course you are, no one can live without all the things that make us happy. I know I would be an absolute wreck if I didn't touch fabrics, see colours and beautiful designs. And you … you need to share what's so important to you – your God vibes."

"Oh God," sighs Devon feeling a lecture coming on.

"Yes, exactly. But fear not, my dear. Today I've come up with a plan." He presents Devon with a flyer.

"Pray and be Gay?"

"Yes, isn't that the point? To pray so that we can be gay, gay, gay?" he laughs. He has made a flyer announcing an informal church meeting. It includes the venue (Devon's house), a time (this evening) and the name of a priest (Devon) on the flyer.

"Oh my God, you didn't distribute this or anything, did you?"

"I did. But I was thinking we could keep it light, you know, nothing too churchy," he adds.

"I told you that I left the whole churchy-thing behind."

"But you don't want to, and you don't *have* to. You shouldn't have to." He pauses. "Listen, be gay, be a priest, they don't have to be incompatible terms, Dev. I mean, maybe that's your 'calling' you know." He makes the quotation marks in the air. "Just grab it by the balls! I mean, at the end of the day, what the hell are rules anyways? They're just things that people make up to feel safe. You don't need a church. You can make your own."

"No, absolutely not!"

"Well, the flyers are out, Devon – are you?"

Owen fusses that there aren't enough chairs in the house; he has slipped a flyer under every door within a two-block radius. Devon walks out onto the stoep. He is done trying to talk sense into Owen. It is already eight o' clock and no one has arrived.

"Damn, these bleddy whiteys," says Owen. "At least in my old area people would have come just for a show and some gossip. Can you possibly be so uncurious about your neighbours?"

Devon takes in the quiet stars; the balmy air lends a decadence to a moment that could not be more splendid. He shifts closer to his man who, with the grace of a clown, tried to move heaven and earth for him.

Shejal pauses with hands on top of the kitchen counter as his stomach cramps and groans. As the intensity of the cramp passes, he decides to eat. He opens the fridge and digs into the miscellaneous containers for leftovers; a little bit of dhal and some rice, then some noodles. It is only once he is done shovelling food into his mouth that his eye catches the clock. This meal is not dinner, as he imagined; it is three 'o clock in the morning. Life is now an erratic rotation of work, sleep and food; the skeleton of time and the firm-bodied security of knowing and judging the hour by where one is and what one is doing, no longer exists. He had only planned to take a short nap before dinner.

He eats quickly, though nothing tastes like food anymore. Even so, once he is done, he returns to stand in front of the fridge as if pleading with his palate to decide what it needs next to end this episode. He slices off a chunk of cheddar cheese and minces it between his teeth. At the height of frustration, he butters a slice of bread and stuffs in into his mouth. His jaws are already sore from chewing and the bread turns into an emulsified blob in the back of his throat.

✳

"Mummy's coming back! Mummy's coming back!" screams Amy.

Janine looks at her pitiably. Amy is always wishing that her Mummy will come back. "But your mother is in Australia," she says, trying to be as tender as she can.

"No. No! She is flying back and we are going to be a family again. She loves me! She loves Daddy," she says, and throws a scatter cushion straight at Janine's face.

"Just come and sit and have your breakfast."

Janine shovels her muesli and milk into her mouth and chews the cud of Amy's revelation. It is hard to tell fact from fiction with children. She does not move from the table as she waits the two hours that it takes for the captain to come home.

"How was golf?" she asks snidely. She tidies up the table for him to have his breakfast. "Would you like something to eat?"

"No. I don't want anything. I already ate."

"Oh," she says, "anything else you care to tell me?"

He laughs, always finding it difficult to deal with her moods.

"You know, Amy is always singing about her mother coming home," says Janine. "I really think you should sit with her and talk about that." She looks up at him for a response. She watches him pour out some cereal into a bowl. She watches him pour in some milk.

"I thought you said you already ate?" She watches him make extra effort with his jaws to show that he is chewing. She catches his spoon in mid-air and flings it to the floor. "I thought you said you already ate!"

"I meant to say something … but I didn't want to say anything until everything was finalised. But yes, yes, your services are no longer required."

"My services!" she shouts. "My services?"

"Yes," he says, "in about a month or so. She says she misses home, the family, and she wants to try again."

As he works arduously, insistently, on her body, Neha stays pinned to the bed, trying to distract herself from what already feels self-evident: in giving himself so completely, she is left with nothing to grasp at – he has bridged the gap of desire and closed its gate.

"Kathlego, I can't. I can't anymore," she stammers.

He laughs and kneels on the bed, waiting for her to suggest some other form of play instead.

"No, no!" she says as he leans in to kiss her thigh. "I know," she adds softly, cryptically.

"What?" he asks gently, always intent on listening to her.

"We have built warm, damp caves in each other's hearts," says Neha, trying to explain the depth of safety she feels in his strong, long arms, "but I look at you and I know you are hiding in a cave – in the darkness – to protect yourself from the world."

Kathlego blinks profusely. "But, but …" he says, "*this* feels safe. You feel safe, Neha."

"Maybe our hearts don't actually *want* to be safe."

"Maybe our hearts don't want to be alone."

"I feel like a baby stifled in the womb," she adds venomously, feeling resentful at having to shoulder responsibility for his pain.

Kathlego blinks at the blow. "Hayi, Neha," is all he can say.

Suddenly she pulls him into a tight embrace; now she understands the depths of tragedy – it is not being happy in the resting place. How silly it feels, counterintuitive even, to rip this apart so that they might dash forward, to suffer the wounds of work and passion.

"Why, why?" he pleads in earnest.

"To fill a void is to put the cork on a bottle of wine. To love is to spill it."

Govind started renovating their house when Kumari insisted on starting their family. Her despair is now marked by each brick as his monument is slowly and successfully erected, while her plans have failed to spring to life. She feels relieved at the sight of him asleep, not missing a moment of his flaring temper. She does not dare to wake him to share her news. Hope shines in her womb.

She pulls on her gown and travels up the staircase of the almost complete double storey extension to their home. She tramps on the cold, crude concrete floor and gazes at the taut wooden beams upon which a roof will soon be placed. As they draw tall shadows across her body, she grips the soft flesh of her belly and offers it up to the stars. The gratitude she feels brings easy tears to her eyes. She has been dreaming of Elina every day, and she feels certain that a gift of this magnitude could only come from her. The stars are like small bodies of light beaming in the dark sky and summoning her. Now entrusted with their gift, they are asking her to journey further still into their blazing corridor of fire. She pulls a dirty plastic sheet to the centre of the room and covers it with the cheap blanket that she finds there. Like a bird building a nest, she scrunches the two together and lies down on this rudimentary bed. She gazes up at the stars and watches them attentively as they map out the way home. She soon falls asleep, gathering energy for what looks like a long and difficult road ahead.

✳

Janine lets herself in with the key that she kept meaning to return, but that she never seemed able to persuade herself to remove from the keyring.

"Janine!" says Neha.

She lays her bag down to free her hands for an overdue embrace.

"Shejal is such a mess," says Neha.

"So am I," she says, "so am I."

She goes to Neha's room, dives straight into the bed. They curl together tightly to form a Siamese body of overlapping arms and unnecessary organs as they breathe synchronistically: Neha in, Janine out – Janine in, Neha out.

"Do you know what I have done? Where I have been?" asks Janine.

Neha feels her insides rattling like a door on a furnace as it holds back a roaring heat. "Shh," she says, not willing to give shame a voice, "my sister."

✳

Shejal has completely ignored Janine since her return and they are all astonished, if not afraid, when he turns up at the dinner table, breathless and flushed. But he has been given no option, he requires an audience.

"Kumari phoned me at work today. She says she is coming home, back here," he frets, not bothering to take a seat.

"What?" asks Neha.

"She's, what, coming with Govind?" asks Devon.

"I don't know," he moans, "she called me at work and said that she is coming back with her plus one and that we should be prepared. She gave me strict instructions to pick her up from work in two weeks' time and bring her back here. She said it can't be sooner. She has to get everything ready."

"Is she alright? We should call again, make sure," says Janine.

Shejal does not answer, he remains preoccupied. Her voice was tense, low; she whispered into the mouthpiece – no doubt from her open-plan office – and refused his offer to come over to see her. "Not yet," she said. Yet, despite the whisper, she sounded decisive and firm, more than she had in years.

"Let's give her the benefit of the doubt, let's leave her plan as she's set it," he decides.

"Gosh, where do we put everyone?" asks Neha.

ETHER

April 2003

Kumari sighs as she feels all her weight drop into the chair.

"Here you go," says Janine, propping the cold glass of iced tea into her hand. "Since you quit your job you'll be able to take all the time in the world to be with your baby before you hunt for another job. That's cool, hey?"

"Oh, ja, I guess so," she responds lazily.

Her eyes flit like butterfly wings. She gives into the lull of an extraordinarily warm Saturday afternoon and lets sleep snatch pieces of her existence.

Janine adjusts the fan and tiptoes out of the room.

There is a drill ringing outside. She shifts the curtain away from the front room window and looks up at Shejal on a ladder, attaching brass numbers to the front of the new house. She watches his teeth clench and his arms turn into steel as he holds the drill in place. His face is dusted with paint and plaster. His grubby T-shirt sticks to the sweat collecting on his back. He has almost single-handedly finished all the work on the house in his spare time. He has painted, oiled, filed, sawed, cut, drilled and screwed everything into place. As a result, he has lost a lot of weight. She wonders if this is what he really needed – a project – to fix a house and himself in turn.

"Hey … I thought you might want something to drink?" she asks shyly, coming outside. "I wasn't sure if you wanted some," she says as she holds out a glass of iced tea. It perspires in her hand, sending beads of water running over her knuckles.

"Thanks," he says, climbing down.

Janine shifts the glass into his palm and turns on her heels to leave.

"Wait, wait," he says. He gulps the drink down and hands the glass back to her.

"Do you want some help?" she offers, as she has many times before.

They both turn towards the street at the sound of momentum. A small coloured girl and boy race each other along the road on their plastic motorcycles. Their limbs bend like frog legs as they paddle along the ground. The plastic wheels grate against the loose gravel on the tarred road and send them into dangerous sideways angles. They giggle and cheer, oblivious to the injury that possibly awaits them.

"I don't have anything else to do," she adds.

"You can hand me the numbers so that I don't have to come back down from the ladder every time," he suggests, watching the children make it safely all the way to the bottom of the street.

"Okay, cool," she says, keeping the surprise out of her voice. She eagerly hands him the brass plates: a 1, another 1, a 7, a 0, an 8, and a 6. The area is new, and people still use plot numbers instead of street numbers to mark their houses in this new extension in Lenasia. All the houses are built alike; small, box-like and affordable, part of the government's cheap housing scheme. But already their house is the anomaly of the area – Devon bought it from the previous owner, who had bought the neighbouring house as well and built a double storey in its place. It is big enough for all of them without the need for extensions.

"There we go," says Shejal as he climbs down to see if the numbers are straight. "117086 Eastside Avenue."

Janine can hear the ring in his voice. He is home.

"Well," she says as silence extends into awkwardness.

She has already made the journey back to Never Never Land to face the wrath of Mrs Walters. With no defence, she humbly said "yes" to all accusations and so she is back at her job, but Shejal is clearly much less forgiving of her desertion. She has thought about climbing into his bed during the middle of the night, though seduction has already proved to be an inaccurate missile to aim at someone's heart. Yet now in the warmest of fantasies, all she keeps seeing is Shejal's hand planted on her back; firm, secure and reassuring. It is often enough to make her jolt from her seat.

"Well," she says again before she picks up his empty glass and goes indoors, leaving him to stand and stare at the house.

"Oh, can I have some of that?" asks Devon with a look at the glass in her hand. His hands are caught under the sofa as he and Owen push it all around the living room. "I told you it was fine where we had it," he says.

They step back to assess the placement.

"No, no, it's still not right," says Owen. He throws his hands up in the air. They have been trying to find the perfect spot for this couch for the last hour – nothing seems to work for him.

Both of them flop down. Janine cannot help laughing as she returns with their drinks. They sit with the pretence of anger on their faces as they try to win the other over with their décor sensibilities. Devon slaps Owen on the wrists. The slap is so girly that Janine knows it must come out of Owen's repertoire. He is, as he keeps saying, "helping everyone to embrace their inner queen".

He even tried his luck with Neha. Just last week, he cupped his hands around his mouth, made the sounds of a siren to indicate the spot inspection of the fashion police and busted her cupboard open. He confiscated the shoddy pair of jeans that she has worn since she was 13. He then took her for a drive and brought her home with her hair chopped into a neat bob that is now much too short to be tied into a ponytail anymore.

"I like it here," says Owen finally as he stacks his empty glass into Devon's.

"I like it here too."

"I'm talking about the couch, dear," says Owen drolly.

"So am I!" exclaims Devon, glad that they've come to an agreement.

❋

"Well, goodbye, Dad," says Neha. "No, no, don't worry. I'll let myself out," she adds.

His steps are no longer so strong, the grip on his whiskey glass no longer certain. Her father has become an old man, she accepts this, retirement leaving him to wallow in time and space. She gets into her car and takes the two-minute drive from her parents' house to hers. She feels relief at being so close to them. The very same intimacy of space that horrified her in her youth, now gives her great comfort. As she sees Kumari's belly grow and her back groan with pain, she understands the extent of the sacrifice she imposed on her mother's body and learns the fear that she must have evoked in her father's heart – fear of whether the world, as harsh and cruel as it can be, would allow for something as fragile as a baby. Now as the time approaches, she accepts that she is here to usher her parents into death, just as they once brought her across the threshold, to life.

She turns in at Extension 13 and makes her way along the narrow squiggle of streets towards the place she now calls home. It sits on the fringe of Greater Lenasia, at the very edge, close to the swamp. The ominous thirteenth extension was never part of the initial plan of Lenasia. It is part of the council's scheme to help house the less fortunate people of the country in the cheapest possible way. *The thirteenth extension,* she marvels. *What people were too superstitious and too frightened to build has now been built.*

As she drives through the area, she is pleased that this is not quite the Lenz that she grew up in. She chuckles as the Pakistani boys who always stand on the street corner gawk at her. As much as this area is economically poor, it is imaginatively rich. There is a great sense of making things up in these streets as people improvise alongside and against their cheap and banal off-white houses. The neighbours too are a rich chaos of people from Soweto and Orange Farm, Malawi and Zimbabwe, Eldorado Park and Ennerdale, some Indians from Lenasia and then Indian-Indians and Pakistanis too. Her reference point for the word 'neighbour' has grown so large that Neha thinks it must encompass the world. She has had to travel so far to come so near, for something as small and as vast as this.

"My, my," she says to Shejal, impressed at the shining numbers on the wall. "We should give this house a name. We never did at our last home, but we should give this one a name."

"A name?" he asks, squinting at her.

"Ja, man...You worked so hard on it, why not?"

"Like what? 'The Edge of the Swamp'?" he asks sarcastically.

"Ah ja, you mean like Uhlanga, the originary Zulu marshlands? Ja, that's a good name, and it has a nice ring to it."

He grunts and pulls a face.

"Oh, just sleep on it ... Think about it."

She pats Janine's head on her way in. The girl who still smokes cigarettes on the stoep just so she can be close to Shejal.

※

Devon sits on the bed as Owen folds his clothes meticulously into a suitcase.

"I don't know how you Vaalies survive. The winters are so cold, traffic is so shit and everything seems so dangerous in bleddy Joburg," says Owen with a touch of his old twang, already coming back in time for his trip.

But Devon clicks his tongue, upset that Owen is leaving.

"I don't know. I guess I just miss my family … and its time I out myself," Owen shrugs. "I will come back, you know."

"Oh, I know."

Owen drops his jersey to sit on the bed next to his sullen, sock-folding lover. "You, my dear, have given me love and peace like no other. For the first time, I don't feel like a sadistic fucken bitch. There is no pain, no drama – just love … and good sex," he giggles. "I am coming back!" he shouts into Devon's ear to force him to hear it.

"You see here," he says as he goes over to open the cupboard. He uses his hand to show the empty space and then points to the single item that he has left hanging on the rail: his technicolour dreamcoat. "So you *know* … I'm coming back. There is no chance in hell that I will leave *that* behind," he laughs.

Devon stands up to try on the coat, still mesmerised by the deluge of clashing colours and textures.

"And if you let some other queen wear it and pretend to be me, I will kill you. See?" warns Owen, protective of both his coat and his lover. "You know I ate bread and cheese for two months just to buy that jacket."

Devon laughs at his commitment to his vanity. If Owen's commitment to him is only half as strong, he is in safe hands.

Janine would have thought that Kumari was still asleep were it not for the active flow of tears that run past her shut eyes.

"Kumari!"

The sudden interruption startles her, waking her from her nightmare. "I'm sorry. I'm sorry," she mumbles through her tears.

"What the hell for?"

"Oh, I don't know … anymore."

Janine pulls up a chair and hands Kumari a tissue.

"Do you think he will find me?"

"Don't worry, he can't, he won't," says Janine. "He doesn't have any of our numbers and we've moved houses without a trace. And you haven't been to your parents, or your old job, so there is no way, no way he will find you here."

Kumari still drowns in the shock of the events, her uncharacteristic escape.

"Come now, you did this for a better life, here, with us! You did this for your baby, remember?" she whispers, placing her hand on Kumari's substantial belly.

"Sweetness," she whimpers into her belly, "your mummy better think of some names soon or else this one will stick."

Janine cannot take her eyes off the unborn child. *I see you all the time,* she thinks, *even when I close my eyes and fall asleep, it is your face that I see.* There are no more broken foetuses and black ghosts in her dreams. She indulges herself by planting a kiss on Kumari's belly, letting in the little seeds that constantly germinate in her heart. Kumari is too stupefied by her self-pity to bother reacting, but Janine plants a kiss on her forehead too.

✳

Kumari's heart rails at the world. *This was not how I wanted it to be.* She has so much venom to spit into the eye of God. Months later, it is too embarrassing to confess, but she still toys with the romance of rescue, with the hope that Govind will find her, mumble apologies for his years of negligence and violence, do the work to win her back. But now she has begun to despise herself for it.

243

Janine rearranges and tidies the room in silence, leaving her to cry her ugly, bitter tears. *What a kind and quiet hero,* she thinks. It is Janine who knows all about pregnancy and birth and babies. It is also Janine who has arranged a place for the baby at Never Never Land so that Kumari can return to work as soon as she finds a new job. What a relief to have so much of the pressure of being a good mother so graciously taken from her, at least until she pushes through the charred soil in her heart.

She hears Mapaputsi's "Kleva" being spit from a crackling speaker. Sure enough, she stands at the window and sees a familiar Sunday routine playing itself out. Jabu, their neighbour, sits on rusted oil drums with a quart of beer at his feet. Joanna, his wife, carries their baby around on her hip and walks barefoot in the cemented yard. Mother and child wave at her and Joanna yells for her to come down for a visit, but she waves them off, nowhere near ready to join the company of people who have fallen so easily into the happy rhythm of their young nuclear family.

Devon puts on a fresh shirt and the starchy crispness of the collar beguiles him as it grazes his neck. Everything that crosses his path seems to burst with abundance. The flowers say "good morning" in their pots, the bright green lawn that Shejal planted over the sand glistens with dew, the taste of toffee is on his tongue and he strokes the smooth knot of his silk tie. Owen has departed on his journey, leaving enough time for Devon to contemplate his own under the guiding hand of God. It is like falling in love again; it makes him giddy with joy. All of life rings in his body like a pregnant womb. It ripples with the same active vibrations that dance across Kumari's outstretched belly.

Men make such a narrow thing of freedom, he thinks. As if freedom itself is about travelling absolute roads going one way or the other. Human freedom, as he sees it, gave him the option to go gay, go straight or go home (all the way to hell – not omitting the option of suicide). None of which are suitable answers for him. He will *have* to make his own answers… *This is* my *freedom,* he thinks, in awe of his God who, like the regal Sheba, makes a fool of any man with a plan. He scoffs with delight. The gospel of Christ, as his heart instinctively knows it, is always a case of mutatis mutandis under which there exists no anomaly. Today Devon walks towards his shitty Corolla, it will need time to first cough and then start. Today he strolls back into a church he once fled.

※

There is still the matter of the skirting board in the lounge that needs to be knocked back into place and the new windows in the kitchen that have not yet been lined with putty, but Shejal surrenders to the exhaustion from the odd jobs that never seem to end. He invests so much energy into the house; this raw and naked shell. Unlike his parents' house, this one does not prescribe *how* to live in it. This house, as it found them and they it, barely had a coat of paint on it – a part of someone else's broken dream. It is late at night and the house is bathed in silence. He tiptoes across the passage to Janine's bedroom and although the door is ajar, it creaks slightly when he nudges it open.

A sheet lies untidily across her body despite the heat. He smiles, knowing she cannot fall off to sleep without something to cover her. Unable to snatch her in his arms, he edges forward and places his palm on the small of her back. She stirs slightly and mumbles as she incorporates him into whatever dream she is having. His head touches the dark tendrils of hair, black as coal and just as shiny. *I have made you my moon, my dark place to hide*, he thinks sorrowfully as he sees the awful burden he has placed upon her, *and when you made decisions I didn't like, I abandoned you.* His palm takes on the same temperature as her skin. He knows that he can never love her as before – she is a part of his broken dream, but also of one he cannot yet understand.

✳

Neha pulls a tight Alice-band across her head. It is the only thing that keeps her hair out of her face, and she laughs at her reflection as she sees her hair sprout from over the band like the wild crest of a wave. She settles down to read, accepting the seclusion of her life in limbo. There is a keen and raw vulnerability to it; jobless and alone. She has submitted her thesis for examination and awaits further pronouncements to be made about her future. In what feels like a timeless reality, she has gone back to the archives and has started researching the history of Lenasia and its inimitable founding father, Captain Lenz. Neha enjoys writing what feels like a useless chronicle – for the historical records on Lenasia are paltry and force her into the role of a fabulist. Her latest research has uncovered that Captain Lenz, after whom their area takes its name, is more of a myth than a man. Instead, she has discovered that *lens* means 'halfway' in Greek and that the name of the area was given by a German communist who joked – who *joked* – that this area is so full of Indians that it is halfway to Asia. They were a people who had nowhere to go and nowhere to come from. *No wonder adventure has evaded us all our lives*, she thinks.

It dawns on her that an entire night has passed without sleep. She opens the window and flicks a lizard from the sill, clearing away this ancient harbinger of false prophecies so that new stories can come. She stands flush against the pane to embrace the cold breezes of the early light. The soft purple haze moves across the bordering marshy lands. As she stares out from her second-storey bedroom, a helicopter zooms in from the far right. It rips across the sky and its blades make undulant waves across the reeds as it lowers over the dense swamp. The searchlight hovers over this familiar hiding spot for thieves that are on the run from the police. But after three circles, the search is abandoned, as usual.

Jairam howls, on alert after the noisy intrusion. Neha pats his head and coos lovingly to appease him. To live anywhere in South Africa is to make a virtue out of the stark awareness of danger. She knows that her choices have to be braver and her love more evident. There is already a group of people standing at the side of the bridge as they throw cremation ashes into the little slip that counts as a river here. Slowly, Neha's attention shifts as the reeds start to *quiver* – the word itself cracks in her mind like the soft ribcage of a bird in a curling palm.

"Jus soli," she whispers. "What will the soil make of us? What will it make of our children?" she asks the wind.

Acknowledgements

I started this book a long time ago and reaching this point is an equally significant story because of the many generous people it includes. I would like to thank my parents for making space for this book – and its author – even when my professional pursuits seemed flighty at best. I'm also deeply grateful for Kama Maureemootoo, Pamela Nichols, Kgaogelo Kwes Shaft Lekota, who all read early drafts of this novel. This book found its home in the Modjaji fold, and I feel so fortunate to debut in such estimable company. Many thanks to Colleen Higgs for taking a chance on me and the Five, Karen Jennings for editing with surgical dexterity and Rudi de Wet for a book cover that makes my heart dance.

I am so honoured to form part of the UCAPI team (Urban Connections in African Popular Imaginaries, Rhodes University), whose constant support feels like sunshine in my soul. I'd also like to express gratitude for book grants received from the Faculty of Humanities, UP and the NRF. The front matter about the history of Lenasia is taken from the Lenzinfo website; Captain Lenz lives on in the virtual realm.

Lastly, writing often puts you in diametrical opposition to the world and to my surprise and delight, my family and friends have not deserted me! Cheryl, Lee-Ann, Kumeran, Heema, Sarona, Thammy, Miriam and Linda thanks for letting me pick your brains, bathe in self-pity when needed and for showing me how life and love outside of the novel are always, incomparably, better.

Printed in the United States
By Bookmasters